BOBOLO:
MAN OF MIRTH

BOBOLO: MAN OF MIRTH

JULIA COOLEY ALTROCCHI

Edited by Paul Hemenway Altrocchi, MD

and

Catherine Altrocchi Waidyatilleka, M.Ed.

Library of Congress Control Number: 2020923394
ISBN: Hardcover   978-1-6641-4363-0
                 Softcover   978-1-6641-4362-3
                 eBook   978-1-6641-4361-6

Print information available on the last page.

Rev. date: 11/23/2020

To order additional copies of this book, contact:
Xlibris
844-714-8691
www.Xlibris.com
Orders@Xlibris.com
822184

CONTENTS

This book is dedicated to
MIRTH —
a condition of supreme
well-being, happiness
and laughter.

"Mirth is God's Medicine.
Everybody ought to bathe in it."
- Henry Ward Beecher, 1813-1887
Minister and Social Reformer

"With mirth and laughter,
let old wrinkles come."
- William Shakespeare
The Merchant of Venice (I.i.80)

Chapter 1

STOP SHAKING MY BED

"Bobolo! Bobolo! Stop shaking my bed! *Santo Cielo* (for Heaven's sake), what are you doing? Son of the devil, answer me! You … you ... *Aiee … Aiee … Aiee*!"

Fiammella's voice, which had begun in the harsh register of rebuke, ended on a long shrill note of terror, as her bed — which had been jolting violently — slid across the room and struck smacko against the west wall of their home in San Francisco. Bobolo, the accused, had already jumped out of their troubled marital bed and was rapidly putting on his trousers while answering his wife's customary reproaches.

"For once this son of the devil isn't responsible, *carissima moglie* (beloved wife)! It's an earthquake, and a big one," said Bobolo.

"Un terremoto? Aiee ..." Fiammella cut short her shriek and rushed from the bed. "The *bambini!* The *bambini!*"

In the corner of the room, their four year-old son Tranquillino lay blissfully asleep. Now as the house began to shake again, the beams to creak, the plaster to fall, and bottles, dishes and pans to crash in the kitchen, the two little girls, Beatrice and Laura, scurried in from their adjoining bedroom.

"What is it, Mama? What is it, Papa? Who's shaking our house?" asked Beatrice.

"It's nothing to be afraid of," answered Papa reassuringly. "Only an earthquake. I felt them plenty in Florence when I was a little boy. It's just that our old earth gets bored rolling around with nothing to do and suddenly takes a notion to kick up a little excitement and burst out laughing! That's all. But I think we'd all better go out to the backyard and stay away from the house until our old earth recovers her dignity."

Bobolo took charge efficiently and bundled his family outside into the backyard. One could hear the excited shrieks and loud talk of other Italian householders along Telegraph Hill and the tumble of dislodged plaster and bricks from damaged houses. The deep subterranean rumbling of the temblor was still reverberating against the gray air of morning.

Dawn shortly began to spill its first sulfur light over the seven hills of San Francisco on that tumultuous morning of the eighteenth of April, 1906. A passing aviator, if aviators had been around San Francisco Bay in those days, might have looked down and observed the many-towered wedding-cake houses on Nob Hill nodding their turrets to one another in fashionable curtseys, the business buildings downtown swaying uneasily, and the little cottages on Telegraph Hill dancing a rapid folk dance. From the crumbling plaster, light plumes of gray smoke and dust swirled up from every hilltop.

Down in the tiny garden bright with tulips, marigolds and yellow acacia at the rear of the Bonomo Italian Grocery and home, Bobolo Bonomo was masterfully taking charge, his auburn hair and red mustache bristling with authority and energy. He permitted no member of his family to return into the house, although the little girls were already pleading for their dolls and canaries, Tranquillino for his toy fire engine and Fiammella for her sewing machine and the precious trunk which contained her wedding dress and slippers and the white satin pillow upon which her wedding ring had been borne up the aisle of the *Church of Santissima Annunziata* in Florence on their wedding day in 1897, nine years before.

Bobolo ventured valiantly into the house and brought forth all these treasures. From the jumble of overturned cans, barrels and boxes, he selected the most essential foodstuffs and carried them quickly by bushel basket into the center of the backyard. Then he went back for his precious casks and flasks of wine. Indeed, he was a committed friend of Bacchus and, as an Italian, he loved his grapes.

Fiammella, who usually issued rather strident, high-pitched orders to Bobolo, was singularly silent, subdued not only by the earthquake but by her husband's instant proficiency in this extraordinary situation.

While Bobolo was carting out his salvaged wines, his best friend, Pio Passerino, a Florentine like himself, rushed through the house into the back yard to see how his friend was faring. Pio was of an undeviatingly orthodox turn of mind, the only feature of his intellect which did not jibe with Bobolo's more supple approach to life.

"Oh, Bobolo! It's the End!" cried Passerino, rubbing his small hands together nervously and cocking his head to one side, for all the world like the sparrow which was his namesake. "It's the Day of Doom! Confess your sins, *mio carissimo amico* (my dearest friend)! And may God have mercy on your soul."

"Figs and fiddlesticks!" declared Bobolo, unloading a basketful of wine bottles a little too vigorously, breaking one of them. "It isn't 'The End' at all, Little Sparrow. It's the beginning of a new adventure! Every calamity is a new opportunity. That's the challenge of life, my friend."

"You'd better be thinking of your sins, Bobolo."

"I've got better things to think of. Besides, I'm not sure I have so many sins to confess. A few indiscretions perhaps, but no sins. Sin is a relative term, *caro amico*. Sins are more vital than virtue, perhaps even more virtuous than virtue."

"Don't be sacrilegious, for God's sake, my poor Bobolo. Do save your soul in this solemn moment!"

"You know, Little Sparrow, I'm not so sure that God is always solemn. I have a hunch that He's a colossally merry soul!"

"Don't blaspheme ..."

"Oh, *basta, basta* (enough)! Save my soul for what? Isn't that rather self-centered? I'm saving my family and my wines instead, Passerino. Here, have a drink with me! A sip of chianti will steady your nerves."

"At six in the morning? Remember the Good Book, Bobolo, where Isaiah tells us, 'Woe to those who stay up late at night to rise up early in the morning and run after their drinks till they are inflamed with wine.'"

"Ah, but the same Good Book, my friend, says, 'Eat, drink and be merry!'"

Bobolo picked up a flask of chianti from the heap, flicked open the corkscrew attached to his penknife, uncorked the bottle, fetched two tin cups, filled them with good red wine and toasted his friend. "Here's to your health, Pio Passerino. But if this be 'The End,' as you so dolefully proclaim, may you enter peacefully into heaven with all your sins forgiven and two of God's prettiest angels blowing sweet trumpet notes into your ears forever."

At the moment when the drinking cups touched, another rumble came out of the earth; the tin cups trembled, precious liquid spilled and the two men reeled. Fiammella, holding her children close to her, looked at the two men wavering and bowing like hinged puppets and, even in the midst of her fright and own unsteady staggerings, couldn't help smiling.

"Ah," exclaimed Bobolo. "It occurs to me what an earthquake is, *per Dio*. It's the earth on a binge. Go to it, old Earth! Have a jag! A laughing jag. *Evviva!*"

"Oh come, come," cried Fiammella. "Always talking and waving your arms! If the house falls and the world comes to an end, you must help us, Bobolo. Come and help me now to build a fire to make some cocoa for the children."

"Yes, *cara mia*, certainly. I'll be right with you. *Un momento.*" Then, to Pio, "Ah me, she's always interrupting my thoughts with the distractions of life. I was just about to catch an idea by the tail when, as usual, she caught *me* by the tail. Most truly has it been said, my dear Pio — *Chi disse donna, disse danno* (Who says dame, says damn)! Well, no matter. Here's to you once more, *amico* Pio," he said and drank what was left in his cup.

"Here's to you, my merry-hearted friend. May you repent of your few sins," Pio replied, and downed the last sip in his tin cup.

"May I never repent the pursuit of a happy life! *Viva la gioia* (Long live joy)! *Evviva! Viva la terra* (Long live earth)! *Viva la vita* (Long live life)!"

"*Basta! Basta*! That's enough!" cried Fiammella. "Come, get to work!"

"Coming, my beloved, coming."

"Since you are okay, I must be getting back to my own yard," said Pio.

"Wait for me," whispered Bobolo to his friend. Pio gave a nod.

Bobolo helped his wife build a fire and get a few provisions together, then announced, "I think I'll go and see what general damage has been done. I must get to the warehouse to see if it's still standing and, if it is, get some new grocery stock."

"You're leaving me now?" cried Fiammella.

"We're in no danger anymore, my dear. The earth is settling down, getting tired of rebelling. Nothing to worry about. Look after the children. I'll be back when you see me."

"Yes. That's always the way it is. 'I'll be back when you see me!' And now you leave me right in the middle of an earthquake. Was there ever such a man as the one I married?"

"I left you the first time after another kind of earthquake. You remember, Little Flame? The earthquake of your temper!"

"Do I remember? Yes! The morning after our wedding. Wicked man! And now you don't care if the earth cracks open with me and your children in the middle of the backyard and swallows your family right up!"

"Oh, Mama. Will that happen to us, Mama?" wailed eight year-old Beatrice.

"Fine business frightening the children," said Bobolo. "No, nothing will happen, children. Everything will be all right and

I'll be back *subito* (immediately)! Come on, Pio." The two men hastened to disappear around the corner of the house.

The street was unrecognizable, cobblestones skittered and scattered. Small shops and houses along North Beach, being of wood, were still standing but some just barely. Many were chimney-less and broken-windowed, covered with plaster dust as if after a snowstorm.

While many of the Italians, like the Bonomos, had taken refuge in backyards, others were grouped along the middle of the street away from possible falling beams, tiles and timbers, talking quietly now that the wild gesticulations and magpie *ciarlare* (chatter) of the first wild moments of the cataclysm had passed. The possibility of unfinished crustal upheavals hung a weight on the quick pendulum of their Italian tongues. No meaningless verbiage now, just a silent shouldering together during the fearful first hours.

Bobolo moved among the little groups like a scarlet tanager among ravens, leaving spots of brightness wherever he went, from the merry absurdities of his own unfettered tongue. He was known as a great fellow for pranks and practical jokes but he must now use this talent for uplifting the fears and gloomy spirits of his neighbors.

"Good for the digestion, this earthquake, you know, *cari amici*. Knocks the kinks out of your intestines. Cheer up! Old Signora Earth is dancing a rapid folk dance, that's all! Skip and prance to it!" said Bobolo and flung his feet about in a few dance kicks over the twisted cobbles while his compatriots looked on, at first as if he were slightly mad, then to laugh and cry out, "That Bobolo's a crazy one. *Bravo*, Bobolo! *Bravo*. Not even an earthquake can get you down."

"Why should it get me down? *Chi vuol vivere e star bene pigli il mondo come viene*. He who would live and fare well must take the world as it comes."

"But it may be the Judgment Day, Bobolo."

"Who's afraid of that special day? That will be a big adventure when it arrives! But this isn't the Judgment Day. We're all alive! *Dopo il cattivo ne viene il buono.* After the bad comes the good. We'll all help one another repair the houses and our homes will be better than ever!"

"But look at those plumes of smoke! If there's smoke there must be fire. What if the wind brings the fire this way, Bobolo?"

"If fire comes this way, get up on your roofs with pails of water until the hoses come."

"There's no water, Bobolo. The water-pipes are broken."

"No water?" he asked, for a moment taken aback. "Then wine will have to do, *amici!* If it's a question of life and death, our tasty grapes must do the job. Soak your blankets, sheets and curtains with wine and spread them over your roofs and walls! We'll save Telegraph Hill and the North Beach from the curtains of fire with curtains of wine, eh, *amici?*"

"*Bravo*, Bobolo! *Bravo*, Signor Courage, *prendere la palla al balzo* — seize the moment, take the bull by the horns even during a catastrophe.

And word spread down the streets from Italian group to group: "Bobolo's not playing one of his pranks this time. Bobolo's advice is *molto bravo.* He says, 'Save your houses with *vino, amici*, curtains or waterfalls of wine against curtains of fire if the flames come our way.'"

Bobolo headed to the waterfront where he could see that the little puffs of plaster dust and smoke, which had first risen like incense from altars over various parts of the city, had turned to twisting black swirls lined with scorching fire. The freshening wind slanted the swirls forward and puffed sparks over the city. The sight was ominous. Blankets of wine might not serve as an effective shield against such leaping sparks and walls of flame.

He ran back along the waterfront towards Telegraph Hill. Processions of people were already heading towards the great open military drilling grounds of the Presidio and the gardens and safe cool lawns of Golden Gate Park to the north-east of the city. Some people were pushing their belongings in wheelbarrows or pulling them in children's toy wagons. One man, a pair of shoes tied to a stick slung over his shoulder, was as jaunty as Bobolo, walking along singing, "I Can't Think of Nuttin' Else But You, Lulu!"

Bobolo didn't show any outward evidence of worry or anxiety but he had never before witnessed the widespread destruction of such a powerful earthquake. The situation was getting worse and more menacing by the minute. It was definitely time to get his family somewhere to safety and to try to save his house and his belongings. He hurried on, an encouraging look of confidence on his face. As he reached the Italian quarter where he was well known, people began again asking him for advice.

"What shall we do, Bobolo? Do you think the city is going to be destroyed by fire after so much damage already by the earthquake? Where shall we go? Should we stay and try to save our houses?"

"Send your families over to the Presidio and Golden Gate Park, then stay here as long as you can to guard your property. That's what I'm going to do. *Buona fortuna* (Good luck)!"

When, some two hours after he had left home, he returned safely again to the bosom of his family, he found that bosom heaving as usual. It was as an offset to the temperament of his excitable wife, the flamier half of their partnership, that he had hopefully named his little son Tranquillino.

"Good-for-nothing! Do-nothing! *Fannullone!* What have you been doing for the last two hours while San Francisco burns? Fiddling like Signor Nero?" reproached Little Flame, Fiammella, his wife.

"Do nothing? Ha! See the sweat running off my head? I've been climbing over the ruins and barricades, the craters and chasms of the city, my love, to find out how things are, whether we can stay where we are, whether we should take a boat across the bay or whether we'd better go out to the park to save our lives.

Do nothing, indeed! I was almost shot to death for my zeal by a soldier on guard."

"A likely tale. *Il Capitano Fracasso* (loud noise)! Boom, boom!"

Bobolo shrugged his shoulders but a little stab went through his heart for all of the cynical barbs emerging from Fiammella's ill-tempered throat. Didn't she have one tiny little ounce of affection for him? *Mondo cane!* It's a dog's world! Not one ounce?"

"Well, how is it? What shall we do, great sage?" asked Fiammella.

"We're going to stay here just a little longer; that is, you and the children are. Then, if the fire gets worse ..."

The fire soon did get worse. By evening the wind had carried thousands of sparks, lighting dozens of fires. The red-lined clouds of smoke cast a fiery glow that could be seen as a powerful blush on the sky as far south as Monterey. Now the exodus from the city really swelled. The sounds of hordes of people walking and of trucks being dragged by ropes along cobbled streets mingled with the crackle of advancing flames, the detonations of explosions, accidental or purposely set to stop the fires from further advance, and the bark of the rifles and pistols from soldiers and vigilantes against the actions of thieves and looters.

Bobolo equipped his family with sacks of provisions salvaged from the stock of his grocery store, put blankets over their shoulders, and told them he would find them when all danger was over. Leo, their Irish setter, would go with them as protector. He embraced the children and Fiammella lengthily before he let them go. To Bobolo's delight, Fiammella clung to him wildly and affectionately, without any rebuking.

"Ah, Papa, take care! Don't let aftershocks get you or fire burn you!" she begged.

"Ah, but Fiammella, *cara*, how often have you told me to go to the place where one burns through eternity! Many's the time you've wanted a broiled husband, *non è vero* (isn't that true)?"

"*Che grullo! Che stupido! Che insensato*! How dumb! What a stupid fool! What a madman!" screamed Fiammella in her more familiar tone.

"*Addio, cara*, (farewell, my dear). Keep yourself and the children safe," replied Bobolo, smiling.

Chapter 2

WINE AND FLAMES

Bobolo stood and waved until his family group, lighted by the gray-ruddy flames of the burning city, was obscured by other trudging groups. Then he hurried back into the house to make what preparations he could to save their property. Following the advice he had already given his friends, he took all the sheets and blankets that remained in the house, went into the basement, opened the bungs of the wine casks and soaked every inch of the material, cursing to himself all the while for the pitiful waste of the *vino* he had so adored since childhood.

"What a sad time! *Per Bacco* (By Bacchus)! *Porco demonio!* God is behaving like a pig to us! What a waste! Blood of the earth! Great juice of Heaven! Angels and demons, what a squander! Blankets of wine, sheets of wine, lakes and seas of wine! Enough for a thousand carousels with friends! What laughter, what witty words, what world-shaking wisdom might have flowed with the royal purple rivers of this wine, lost now forever in the sheep's wool of these blankets, the silly cottonpuffs of these sheets! What a waste! *Santo demonio!* What a wicked, wicked, heart-breaking waste! The devil can be a cruel companion!"

When the drapes were a rich, grapey purple, Bobolo wrung them out a bit, licked his fingers, then lugged them upstairs in several loads. He set a stepladder against the house and spread soaked blankets and sheets over all of the roof and down as much of the walls as he could. By this time the wind was already carrying deadly sparks from timbered house to house along Telegraph Hill. New leaves of flame were sprouting in the Italian section wherever house-owners had failed to spread their protective cloths of *vino*.

Ash and flaming fireflies were falling ominously in Bobolo's own yard. Cinders drifted down upon Fiammella's precious sewing machine and trousseau trunk. Quickly, Bobolo scavenged flasks of wine from the debris of the shop, then poured from a flask in each hand twin streams of violet over his wife's two most prized possessions. Being a fellow of imagination, he knew what a ludicrous picture he made and how he would describe the scene later to his friends, when wine could slowly be poured down throats again, not flung over objects incapable of appreciating it!

The personal possessions of his wife, resting beside the heap of canned goods and wine flasks, were palpably feminine and he was struck, now of all times, by faintly tingling romantic associations. Inside that trunk lay Fiammella's wedding dress. A handsome girl she'd been, flashing-eyed, a mettlesome filly from Florence! He, Bobolo, was born in Florence in 1872. He immensely enjoyed studying history and literature at the University of Florence for two years but had to drop out for financial reasons. He then spent two years learning the hotel and restaurant business, met the spirited, beauteous but sometimes headstrong and sharp-tongued Fiammella when she was twenty-two and he was twenty-four. One year later, on September 20, 1897, they married in Florence, he being under the youthful Shakespearean illusion that he could quickly tame her of any shrewishness. Pitiful underestimation! He had had to give up that hazardous enterprise in the first few hours of marriage.

After consummating their marriage on the wedding night, they had a vehement exchange in the wee hours when, under the influence of much too much champagne, she suddenly turned on him in attack-mode. Although she had previously mentioned a handful of her many boyfriends since age sixteen after she won the Annual Florentine Beauty Contest, she had told Bobolo repeatedly that she had blocked every attempt at physical interaction by her many gentlemen friends. Kissing yes; anything else, no. *Niente, nulla*, nothing. She was a virgin, yes, for sure — pristine and untouched.

Fiammella liked her wine but rarely drank anything stronger. At the wedding reception she was in a joyful mood and drank one glass of champagne after another, despite a warning from her mother, who had been watching and knew too well her daughter would regret over-indulging. The happy bride was staggering a bit but giggling when she and Bobolo finally left the reception at midnight and retired to their hotel honeymoon suite. In the privacy of their shared room, she and Bobolo toasted their union with two more glasses of champagne. A mistake, to be sure. At last, she nudged her new husband towards the bed. As he leaned in to kiss her, she urged him rather crudely to "do it" so they could finally experience what they had long waited for. He was certainly ready, awkward and unseasoned. In a whirlwind, the marriage was consummated … far, far too quickly for Fiammella.

"That's it? It's over?" she asked. "After waiting all these years … that's it?"

His face inflamed, he stuttered an apology and quickly tried to reassure her that he could become a good lover in time, if she would be patient.

But her inebriated fuse was lit and she blurted, "Love-making should go on for hours, not seconds! Are you really Italian? *Hah!* My other lovers were far better than you!" With a disdainful snort, she turned from him, sank her head into her pillow and almost instantly began to snore.

Paralyzed by shame and shock, he could hardly believe the stinging explosion from Fiammella. Layered on chagrin over his own performance was disbelief. Did Fiammella, after repeatedly claiming virginity, just unload a champagne-induced bomb? He had only asked her once but she had stated definitively, sworn that she rebuffed all physical advances from men except an occasional kiss. She was a pure virgin. Ice crept through his body as he realized she must have had many lovers, probably beginning when she was sixteen! Alcohol may perhaps cloud her memory of what she just told me, he thought, but I will never forget this revelation — multiple intimate partners — or her impugning my masculinity and ethnic origins.

What had I married? Why in God's name did I talk her into marriage so soon, with only a month being engaged! Her parents, certainly aware of her past lovers, urged us to move slowly, to get to know each other better. Waiting awhile for such a serious step as marriage would be prudent, they repeatedly advised. Why didn't I listen to them? What other secrets will I unearth about her?

Bobolo spent the rest of his wedding night tossing and turning on his side of the bed, thinking. He would never have dreamed that the current Greco-Turkish war could seem so inviting, that such an armed conflict could have beckoned so boldly, so irresistibly. But no great military battle could be so threatening as an excoriating, venomous bride! He saw his independence suddenly and pervasively throttled, his soul and positive life force stifled forever. What a mistake he had made and what sorrowful lifelong penalties awaited him!

The very next morning he had simply declared, "I want to think things over after your spiteful outburst last night. I will see you when I see you." He marched out and joined other volunteers from Italy, enlisting to fight alongside the Greek Army to keep Crete free from the invading, avaricious, rapacious Turks.

With minimal training, he survived two fierce battles in Crete, including hand to hand combat. He was testing whether God wanted him to die in battle or return to his wild, intemperate bride. He received only minor wounds. Was it time to return to Florence and discuss with Fiammella whether they should stay together and try to make a go of it?

Reflection suggested to Bobolo that perhaps he hadn't taken sufficient time to analyze the pros and cons of his sudden decision to leave her. What wisdom had he acquired during his two years at the University of Florence studying history and literature, including the Greek philosophers? The amazing sequence of post-wedding events prickled his conscience. He decided to give the marriage another try. After three months in the military, he resigned and headed back to Florence.

As to Bobolo's abrupt departure, Fiammella remembered no "spiteful outburst." She was dumbfounded and abashed in front of family and friends to have been left not "at the alter" but *after* the alter. She had lost her voice completely for a month. To inquiries, she silently indicated she knew no reason for him to leave her. She realized she had been inebriated on the wedding night but could recall no details. In her mind, she simply blamed him completely and that was that.

When Bobolo returned home, Fiammella reluctantly agreed to give matrimony another try. She did not ask him what precipitated his sudden enlistment in the Greece-Turkey war, worried what he might tell her. Bobolo wondered why she had told such a powerful trust-breaking lie about her past, her virginity, when such lies rarely stand the test of time? Even Saint Augustine said that once a person lies, he or she is rarely if ever completely trusted thereafter, no matter how many times one forgives the liar. Nevertheless, the pair simply "painted over the rust" and endeavored to begin the marriage afresh.

Fiammella's voice had indeed come back, louder and more strident, multiplied in power, force and mockery. Some day he'd try to figure it all out — why he loved to tease Fiammella with tricks and pranks when they so often engendered her vitriol, why she scolded him so often but every now and then revealed an apparent ardent, underlying devotion to him, why he acted as he did, why she acted as she did.

Pouring wine over the trunk that contained his wife's wedding dress to prevent it from burning after a severe earthquake was no time for deep reflection. Preserve the wedding dress. Preserve the marriage. Preserve life, joy and laughter — the happiness of living. But oh, Bacchus — help me to preserve a reservoir of happiness, good cheer and mirth!

All during that night of raining embers, Bobolo and his neighbors in the Italian colony on Telegraph Hill continued to dribble their precious wine over sheets, blankets and tablecloths. They tried to protect roofs and walls and piled heaps of belongings in backyards and along what was left of disrupted front walks and curbs. The violent earthquake, fire, smoke, scrambling ant-humans and lurid fire glow put Bobolo in mind of what it must have been like in Pompeii when Vesuvius erupted in 79 AD. But here, thank God, there were no fast-moving clouds of gaseous fumes and no deadly smothering layers of blazing hot ash.

The lion-roars of the earth had subsided but there was still the intermittent rumble of dynamite and the staccato sound of guns, as one or another of the thirty marauders and looters of that night were shot down by General Funston's soldier-guards. The flame-crackle was louder than ever, audible in the night at a mile's distance. In the quieter intervals one could feel the mesh of human nerves, stretched like vellum over the drum-head of the shared catastrophe, thrumming almost audibly. Such a hum could again become a universal scream. Bobolo began to sing the absurd song:

> I'm the son of Bacciccia, ah, ah, ah!
> With a mouth as wide as a barn-door, eh,eh,eh!

His voice rose like laughter against a storm, a gull against the wind. In a few minutes, Bobolo's neighbors, working at their wine blankets to the right and left of him, took up the refrain. Soon the melody caught like singing sparks from roof to roof until the entire Italian colony was one voice under the invisible baton of Bobolo's exuberant leadership — fruit shop owners, crab-fleet fishermen, and dock hands right down to the water's edge of San Francisco Bay. Then Bobolo, the impresario, and his unseen chorus ran through all the favorite tunes of the Italian-American community from *Torna a Surriento* through *Santa Lucia* and *Bocca, Bocca Bella*.

It occurred to Bobolo that the famous *Rigoletto* aria, *La Donna è Mobile*, "Woman is fickle, more fickle than the wind," might be a devilishly good song with which to castigate that faithless wind which was still sweeping sparks from roof to roof outside the wine-drenched Italian colony.

By now the silver, golden blend of dawn was resting on the Contra Costa hills, but in San Francisco itself the colors were violet and brown, orange and maroon filtered through pervasive clouds of dove-gray smoke.

Perhaps the coming of dawn, perhaps the lessening of the high atmospheric pressure, perhaps the effect of the group singing *La Donna è Mobile* produced the cessation of the wind. By full morning the air over the city was motionless. Fires still burned but sent straighter columns of smoke spiraling into the sky. There were no more blown embers starting new fires. A quietness had settled on the city.

It required another thirty-six hours before Funston's trumpeters rode through the streets late Thursday afternoon, officially bugling the news that the fires were out. Much of San Francisco had been destroyed but much had been saved to serve as a nucleus to build a new city for the future.

Chapter 3

MOVING TO TUSCANY

It was only four days after the earthquake when loud words broke out again in the Bonomo household.

"But you can't go, Bobolo! You can't!"

"But I can, *davvero* (indeed), *santissima* Fiammella! And I will!"

"Don't call me *santissima* (most sacred), you blasphemer!" replied Fiammella. "You shan't go. You have duties *here!*"

"*Che chiacchierata* (What chattering)! *Santo cielo.*"

The blue and sulfur zigzags of contradiction shot through the sizzling air. Fiammella brought up a new regiment of reasons. "There's work to be done, so much work, and you won't be back until Monday morning. I know very well you won't arrive back on Sunday. You'll sit up all night with Merlo and fiddle and drink and sing. You've a house to finish repairing and a little restaurant to build, if we're going to have a restaurant … and off you go to San Jose to hunt and it isn't even hunting season. You'll be arrested for sure! And besides, think of leaving your wife and children all alone in a house with no windows yet. It isn't safe. We might even be murdered in our beds."

"Have you ever thought, my dear, how comfortable it might be to be murdered in your bed rather than on the street?"

"*Demonio* (Demon)!"

"This is all nonsense," said Bobolo. "There are friends all around you. You're as safe as if you were in the Pitti Palace in

Florence. I'll be back by Monday noon at the latest. As for work, I'll be working, too. I'll bring you back a dozen quail and some fat thrushes and half a dozen rabbits for rabbit pie. Get the oven ready! Goodbye, my love."

Bobolo turned on his booted heel and marched out of the house, his gun in the crook of his arm, his hunting cap pushed to the back of his head, his walk jaunty. Then, maddeningly, Bobolo broke into the song of "The Volunteer's Farewell:"

Addio, mia bella, addio.
L'armata se ne va.
Se non partisse anch'io
Sarebbe una viltà.

Goodbye, my beauty, goodbye.
The ships are riding high.
Should I not, dear, depart,
I'd show a coward's heart.

My treasure, weep no more,
Perhaps I shall return.
But if I die in war,
We'll meet on heaven's shore!

If there had been a workable door available, Fiammella would have slammed it, but the door was still skewed from the earthquake. She went into the house quivering with frustration and rage, as so often. For a while she vented on the inside of the dish pan as she washed the last of the breakfast dishes. A mountain of work to do and out walks Bobolo, the devil-may-care, the devil himself.

Yet, in the middle of the cinders of Fiammella's resentment remained the usual unaccountable spark of admiration. The very independence of the man, voluntarily escaping all the entangling circumstances that would have trapped any other tamer man, making every difficulty luminous, dancing late into the circle of freedom and joy that he always managed to create around himself like a magic ring. What a man! *Che diavolo! Che mago* (What a devil! What a magician)! Hate and love intertwined.

Meanwhile Bobolo, little realizing how this particular expedition was to change his life and create a new setting for his future, caught the train that had again begun to operate between San Francisco and San Jose. He stood on the rear platform looking back at the panorama of his ruined city. Almost a month had gone by since the earthquake. Here and there on the slopes, the trellises of new structures were rising. The color of San Francisco was still ash-gray with shades of rust, rose and purple. Even now a beautiful new city was beginning to recreate itself.

But was it a safe place, a healthy place in which to bring up a family of three children? How soon would the earth crash it down again? This year? Next year? A hundred years? How crowded it looked, a continuous mass of fractured walls, brick heaps and finger-chimneys. No trees, no meadows, no space in which to run, dance, think, be alone with one's pleasant self. He was glad he was going out to the country to be with Merlo, good old Merlo, who looked exactly like his name, a carefree blackbird.

In an hour and a half Bobolo was in San Jose. On the station platform was Merlo, his black mustache curling down then sharply up again, accented by a mischievous smile, his cheerful eyes twinkling like the foam beads on a glass of Asti Spumante.

Merlo whacked his friend on the back and repeated over and over, *"Benvenuto, benvenuto, amico Bobolo* (Welcome, welcome, friend Bobolo)! A fine day we have. Many larks in the sky. Good hunting we will have!"

Merlo was scarcely the intellectual type but for a day in the country he pleased Bobolo completely. He hadn't attended any university nor had he read many books. There could be no in-depth discussions with him about literature or history or philosophy, as with Passerino. But with Merlo there could be sport, music, light-hearted conversation, wine-sipping, good eating and the joy of living — not a bad recipe.

Merlo was accompanied by his dog, Nero, a small spaniel that belied the imperial name in bearing and friendliness. Leo, Bobolo's setter, and Nero were already acquainted but it was obvious that the friendship of their owners was not reduplicated in the canine world.

"If you want another breakfast, Bobolo, my Matilda will be glad to make you one. But she's already packed a good lunch for us, with salami, fried chicken, fruit and good wine to add to the game we shoot — she's always afraid we won't shoot anything and then we'll starve." He gestured to the full knapsack over his shoulder.

The jolly sturdy figure of Merlo's blonde Genoese wife Matilda appeared on the stage of Bobolo's mind. Lucky Merlo! His wife idolized him, never scolded him, though she sometimes teased him with *mio caro nano*, my dear dwarf. She hugged him quite openly and often lifted him joyously entirely off the floor in her enthusiasm. Bobolo had often heard her say, "When my little *nano* must go to San Francees-co I am like to die from the loneliness, and he die, too. We cannot live four hours without the other, we miss each other *so* much."

Their only misfortune was that they had no children. But they had a dozen different kinds of animals and birds, and their house was always full of other people's children.

The two hunters struck out on foot north and west from San Jose, for a time following the sidewalks of the town, out past the white cottages festooned with roses and bougainvillea, then into the open countryside between the hills and on the hills, bright now with purple lupine, blue hyacinth, cream-cups and mayflowers. It was a fine day in the fields and they shot a dozen larks. Two rabbits also went into their knapsacks.

The hunters continued diagonally across the plain that lies between the Diablo Range and the Santa Cruz mountains, turning primarily west towards the Pacific Ocean. They came to the foothills near Warm Springs, loved by the Spaniards, and then hiked upwards to Milpitas and Alviso.

"*Per Bacco*, what a beautiful place this is! Let's go a bit higher, Merlo." They climbed until they were at the plateau-summit of a fair-sized hill, with a half-dozen fine live oak trees gracing the slopes. The view was extensive and peaceful. To the east and south were high, fair-clustered hills like a collaret of pearls; to the west the long plain stretched to the silver gleam of San Francisco Bay. To the north one could faintly discern the far gray huddle of San Francisco as one sees Florence lying like a tiny opal on the gleaming distant Arno from the far-off, pine-dark summit of Vallombrosa.

"*Per Dio,* Merlo, what a place! This is as beautiful as Italy! This *is* Italy! This is Tuscany! I'm going to own this piece of land, Merlo. I'm going to live here, I swear it! Here and now, I swear it!"

"Oh no, Bobolo. Not yet. Not yet. Go slow, go slow, *amico.* Your good Fiammella would have to be consulted on that."

"My good Fiammella would love it ... well, not at first, maybe; she's hard to move, but in the end she'd love it! *Dio mio*, this is so beautiful. What a time we'd have, Merlo, hunting around here whenever we wanted!"

"Yes, my Bobolo, but how would you make a living here?"

"Why, we'd open a little country inn, of course, and all San Francisco would flock to it."

"There wouldn't be enough people to patronize an inn so far away from towns and cities, Bobolo."

"In such a beautiful place? You're mad, Merlo, absolutely mad. All San Franciscans would flock to it. The hilltop is sold, Merlo. It's sold to *me*. I'm going to find out who owns it right away. Come with me, Merlo. Come on, *amico.*"

"Good heavens, man, aren't you hungry? This is the place for our lunch. Come, calm down, quiet yourself. Sit down, Bobolo. Get your little knife out and let's prepare two birds apiece. We'll add them to Matilda's picnic lunch. Get busy. I'll build the fire."

Bobolo relented and brought out from his own knapsack a frying pan, shakers of salt, pepper, dried sage, thyme and rosemary and a little vial of olive oil, which were all part of his traditional equipment for hunting expeditions. The lark breasts soon began to fry and sizzle. The two dogs sat down on springy haunches and taut forepaws, ready to jump towards scraps at a signal.

Merlo brought out his harmonica and began to play cheerfully. The air was warm and soft. A carefree lark sang overhead.

"Ah," said Bobolo. "How could kings ask for more? *Paese ridente* (a smiling countryside), friendship, health, a lark above, larks below, wine in the glass. This is life, Merlo! Ah, this is the life of a king! Who needs anything more?"

True to his declaration of intent, Bobolo wasted no time in the matter of real estate. After the fire was doused and the knapsacks repacked, he did not lean back on the hillside for a half hour's nap in the sun as was his leisurely Italian wont. No, he started down the hill at once with Paul Bunyan strides, heading for the little village at the foot of the hill.

"Hold on, Bobolo! I can't keep up with you." Merlo hurried behind, leaping and jumping like a cricket while the two dogs bounded along, leaping over bushes and barking as they sensed Bobolo's excitement.

Down in the village it took only a little scouting around to find the answers to Bobolo's questions. Two old fellows sitting on the steps of the closed grocery store knew that Mrs. Chichester, or Lady Chichester, as she liked to have herself called, owned the hilltop. She was planning to build a small house there in the shape of an ark to shelter her "when the great Deluge comes." The two old fellows both put forefingers to their temples and swirled them around. Everyone knew who Mrs. Chichester was, the widowed heiress to multi-millions who had arrived from the East a quarter of a century ago and had filled the countryside with strange structures, strange behavior and strange legends.

Her prize structure was the great mansion on the road to Milpitas, where she lived. This house was perpetually in the process of additions and construction to keep all evil spirits away with the sound of hammers pounding all day because Mrs. Chichester was mortally certain that the moment the house was finished, she would die.

The strange mansion contained stairs that led nowhere, upside-down handrail posts, a hundred closets filled with the paraphernalia of beauty and hospitality which were never used, six magnificently equipped kitchens and twenty guest rooms for never-invited guests. Mrs. Chichester lived in solitude except for her servants and the crew of carpenters.

Everyone within a circuit of a sixty miles knew who Mrs. Chichester was. Her house was a Sunday attraction for crowds of visitors, the tourist fees paying for the constant carpentry.

"We're off," said Bobolo, pulling at Merlo's jacket sleeve.

"Where to now, Bobolo?"

"Off to see my new friend, Lady Chichester."

"*Dio mio,* she'll never admit you. She'll never see you. She's a hermit; she never sees anyone."

"Just watch me, Merlo. She'll see me. Do you want to wager on it? How about we bet a nice bottle of chianti, or a shiny newly-minted silver dollar made in pre-earthquake San Francisco?"

"*Troppo facile.* Too easy for me to win but I'll take you on, Bobolo. Keep on making bets like that and I'll no longer need to work."

Bobolo walked like a man heading to his *innamorata* after a year's separation. Merlo trailed a step behind and the dogs barked happily.

In two hours the men arrived at the great gray and white frame house. They stood marveling at the turrets, towers and sloping roofs. "It reminds me of a medieval French chateau," Bobolo uttered as he caught his breath. A high stone wall barbed with close-set iron spikes surrounded it. The great iron picket gate was baronial and forbidding. Bobolo spent several minutes inspecting the gate itself and then its bolting mechanism which yielded at his skilled touch. "Maybe I should become a bank robber," he joked as he unlocked the gate and began pushing it open. Belatedly he saw two large Doberman Pinschers eyeing him ferociously from their nearby guard kennels.

"Contribute two of your larks, will you, Merlo?" Bobolo asked, holding his hand back from the gate. "I need mine for a peace offering to Fiammella. You don't need any peace offering because you have a peaceful wife. Be a good fellow. I'll make it up to you and your good Matilda on our next hunting trip."

"Well, you are getting more *sfacciato* (nervy) every year!" Merlo replied.

"You're right, my friend. It is true. Sometimes I am definitely *sfacciato!*"

Overcome as always by the stronger will of Bobolo, Merlo swung his knapsack to the front, reached in and pulled out two larks. The watch dogs must have scented them, for they leaped forward. Leo and Nero began to bark as the two Dobermans growled, proud and battle-ready. "My God, Bobolo, you're not going in to be torn to pieces by those fanged monsters, are you?"

Bobolo's reply was to open the gate just enough to slip through. Instantly he threw a bloody lark to each dog while speaking cajoling words. "Easy, *caro cane* (dear dog), easy *carino canino*. That's a boy, good boy ..."

Merlo watched from the gate, as if looking at Daniel dulcifying the lions.

"Leave Leo and Nero outside and come in," commanded Bobolo. Merlo shuddered so energetically that his knapsack nearly fell off. "Come in, little blackbird, come in."

Bobolo opened the gate wide enough for Merlo to slip in, shutting it before their own two dogs could slip through. Then Bobolo, tugging at Merlo's sleeve, pulled him to the kitchen quarters of the house.

"It all depends on what we find here," declared Bobolo cryptically. "It's servants' day off so there won't be many to deal with. One or two of the help at most. We've got to hypnotize them, Merlo, just as we did the dogs."

Merlo nodded his head and automatically assented. "*Si, si,*" he agreed, though he didn't understand Bobolo's plan in the least. Bobolo rapped a loud brave knock at the kitchen door. He was ready with a dozen subtle approaches for whatever type of servant might appear, male or female — plush chef, frilly-aproned maid or stalwart butler. Yet he never would have dared to dream of the large, wholly amiable and instantly congenial male cook who opened the door with a "*Dio mio!* How you get in?"

Bobolo embraced him lightly, flooding him with Italian salutations, overwhelming him like a long-lost friend, and allaying all possible suspicions by saying that he, Bobolo, was one of the workmen on the house and Italian at that. How could Bobolo have guessed that Fickle Fortune would be on his side by presenting him with an Italian cook in the kitchen?

"I no remember you but no matter. Come in! Come in! Everybody is out except the old lady. Almost time to cook her supper. But meantime a sip of wine, eh? My name is Tito Ruggero, from Roma, now Chef to the Lady Chichester."

"To you, noble Roman," toasted Bobolo before presenting himself and Merlo with a bowing flourish.

Tito was the soul of hospitality. The wine was sparkling burgundy and he added a plate of *pannetone*, a spicy bread which he took from the ice-box.

After three glasses of tasty wine, Bobolo laid his projected campaign before the puzzled Tito. Mrs. Chichester owned a piece of property that he, Bobolo Bonomo, *must* have, out of all the land in the whole territory of the world, for himself, his wife, his three children and his dog, Leo. He absolutely *must* have an audience with Mrs. Chichester. Would Tito allow Bobolo to cook four larks on the kitchen stove for Mrs. Chichester and take them to her personally, Tito going along to vouch for him as one of the faithful workers on her beautiful home? Would Tito say that Bobolo was devoted to the Great Lady of the house and had gone out into the fields to bring her a savory dish of larks?

With some misgivings, Tito assented, as did poor Merlo from whom Bobolo commandeered the last of his personal store of larks.

Tito and Bobolo concocted the supper, working together smoothly, while Merlo nervously paced the kitchen talking, protesting feebly, kibitzing and frequently getting in the way.

When it came time to enter the one dining room out of five for her dinner, Bobolo sleeked himself up at the kitchen sink, placing one of Tito's chef caps on his head, an apron around his waist and a napkin over his arm. Merlo smiled but rubbed his hands nervously. Bobolo stood straight with feigned assurance, an equal-to-any-occasion look spread over his Florentine face.

A buzzer from the dining room resounded through the kitchen. Tito instantly lifted from the serving table a large silver tray containing smaller silver vegetable dishes filled with string beans à la Hollandaise, artichoke hearts cooked in oil, rosemary asparagus with parmesan cheese, and a Bohemian glass decanter filled with cabernet sauvignon. Bobolo lifted the white and gold platter containing the exquisitely spiced larks set on a bed of wild rice. The two chefs marched in step across the kitchen and through the swinging door while Merlo sank into a chair and poured himself another glass of wine. He expected to see Bobolo shortly hurtling through the door on great gusts of disapproval. Could the intrepid Bobolo master that formidable woman in her own domain?

The room that Bobolo entered was so dazzling white, so elegant, so beautifully appointed that even he, prepared for anything, was astonished. Beamed and beveled ceiling, walls, drapes, carpet, marble mantel, damask tablecloth on an immense table capable of seating thirty guests — all were white. It was only later, in a more minute observation of the layout, that Bobolo noticed that, while the room itself seemed to be normal in every detail, the bouquet of white lilacs and white roses in a large crystal vase on the table were thrust flowers-down into the water, stems sticking out in strange twiggy bundles, flowers showing upside-down through the crystal of the vase.

"Lady Chichester," said Tito. "My friend and I bring you a platter fit for a queen, the queen that you are! This is Signor Bobolo Bonomo, one of our carpenters who is also a talented chef. He greatly admires you and ventured off into the country today to bring you a *squsito* (exquisite) dish of savory larks!"

"Larks? Larks?" exclaimed the queen without any visible sign of approval. She was a woman of sixty-seven years, as strange in appearance as was the mind that underlay her alternating stripes of copper and white hair. Each stripe was about an inch wide, drawn back together in precise curved parallels and twisted into a spirally striped pagoda which lifted some seven inches above the rear of her head. At the very top a white rose was insecurely held by an ivory brooch. It wobbled as Lady Chichester exclaimed again, "Larks? Larks?"

Her clothes and demeanor fascinated Bobolo. He was barely aware that she was wearing a gown of ivory lace as beautiful as a wedding gown. But he did take in the pendant of a diamond necklace with a medallion portrait of a bearded gentleman, the miniature suspended upside down. There might be some sense in that reversal at least, thought Bobolo, for to her eyes looking down, the gent, who must be her deceased "lord," was right side up.

Bobolo held the platter close enough to Lady Chichester for the savory aroma to entice her, as he commented. "Yes, my lady, blackbirds for the king, you know, four-and-twenty blackbirds baked in a pie ... but larks for a queen!"

Lady Chichester drew the platter a little closer with a be-ringed finger and sniffed. There were still doubts in her mind. As he watched her, Bobolo noticed her blue eyes. They seemed to change color with the changing thoughts in her mind. From a listless blue they sharpened to sapphire and faded back again. Now they were again sapphire. "That may be," observed Mrs. Chichester, "but what larks are left to sing for the queen if you shoot them all out of the sky?" And she smiled like a shrewd old lady. "Take them away."

"But, Lady Chichester," urged Tito. "We have worked so hard on them to please you. We have spent our Sunday afternoon perfecting them. They are seasoned with rosemary, sage and thyme. They ..."

"Take them away, Tito!"

On her head, the rose nodded. The pendant trembled. Looking at the upside-down image of Mr. Chichester, Bobolo had an idea. "Did you know, Lady Chichester, that larks are very, very unhappy flying around the world right side up? It is only when kind and gracious people like yourself take them in, adopt and consume them, that they can cruise around the world upside-down."

"Set the platter down again, Tito. What did you say your friend's name is?"

"His name, my Lady, is Signor Bobolo Bonomo."

"How do you do, Bo-no-no." She moved a lark breast to her plate, dissected it daintily, brought a forkful to her mouth and began to chew. She paused, savoring it. "This little bird is indeed truly delicious. Come, little pet, you shall fly happily upside down in my stomach."

Bobolo feared to break the spell. She "adopted" all four birds while the chefs stood silently by. When she had eaten the last morsel, she spoke. "Well, Bo-no-no, that's the best batch of larks I've eaten since a dishful I had at a *rosticceria* in Rome thirty years ago with my dear husband. I can hear them singing inside me ..."

"It was a pleasure to prepare them for you, my Lady, a pleasure." He gave the sentence the obsequious but expectant inflection that waiters use to indicate that the service is not yet concluded until crowned with a gratuity. She caught on. She leaned back in her chair and for the first time really looked at Bobolo. His infectious smile made his red mustache almost incandescent.

"What can I do for you, Bo-no-no? Ask whatever you want and it shall be done."

Now that the triumph was at hand, Bobolo knew that he had to *frapper fort et frapper vite*, as the French say — strike hard and strike quickly. "Just one small thing, my lady, just one small thing I would request, if it please you."

"Yes, what is it, Bo-no-no? What would you have me do? No one shall say that the Lady Chichester is not generous to the Man of Larks."

"There is one thing you *can* do for me, my dear Lady Chichester. While hunting this afternoon we came upon a piece of property you own on a hilltop, the place where you are going to build an ark. I'd like to buy that land from you. You would, of course, reserve a building lot big enough for your ark. I'd guarantee to be custodian of the ark, looking after it. That piece of land is a perfect home-place for my wife and three children. It's a hilltop just like the beloved Tuscan hills where I was born."

"Well, well, well … Let me think, Mr. Bo-no-no Lark …"

Bobolo intently watched the color of her eyes. They remained dark blue and rationally focused. "Well," she continued. "I think that's something I can do. A queen never goes back on her word. I promised you whatever you wanted. Bring me my inkstand, pen and a piece of paper from the red library, Tito. Yes, I will sell the hilltop to you, reserving, of course one plot for my floatable structure. When the waters of the deluge come rolling in from the Pacific, I must be safe in my ark."

"Of course, Lady Chichester!" Bobolo felt like dancing a *tarantella* there on the white rug but he restrained himself. Written word to show to her real estate agent was essential. Was this too good to be true? Would the intelligence stripe in Lady Chichester's mind last long enough to get her signature? He watched her eyes. He poured wine for her and urged her to drink it. Her eyes seemed to deepen to indigo.

"Ah, Signor Bo-no-no, you're a smart man and a good man. Could you not stop your carpentry work and be Tito's assistant chef? I'll pay you good wages."

"Not now, my Lady, but I'll bear it in mind. Thank you for the invitation. However, I will come over and cook larks for you whenever you wish!"

This would indeed be something to tell Fiammella whenever she might accuse him of laziness. Any day, any hour, he could land a job in the household of a multi-millionairess!

Tito returned with paper, pen and ink. Mrs. Chichester's eyes remained bright blue as she wrote instructions to her agent in San Jose authorizing him to sell for a reasonable sum her "ark lot" near Alviso to one Bobolo Bonomo (Bobolo carefully supervised the spelling of his name), the bearer, who promised in return to give her, Lady Chichester, shelter in her floatable ark built on a separate piece of land she'd keep for herself for whenever The Deluge occurred.

As she came to the signature, her hand faltered from the effort and, as she looked up, Bobolo saw that her eyes had paled to aquamarine. He quickly handed her the glass of cabernet in front of her. "Drink this, please, dear Lady. It will bring Italian good fortune to our transaction." She did and he took a sip of his own wine.

After the sip, she scrawled her name. He kissed her hand.

An hour later, after a good supper in the kitchen, Bobolo and Merlo set back out through the back yard. Bobolo had forgotten all about the watch dogs but they hadn't forgotten about Bobolo. They made a bound while he and Merlo raced for the gate. Merlo slipped through in time but Bobolo's knapsack was torn from his back by the saber-toothed canine gate guardians, as was a souvenir piece of the seat of Bobolo's pants. Fragments of left-over chicken and salami fell into the paws of the eager devourers. Bobolo kept walking, this time with a broad smile, content that although his pants had lost the second round, the battle victory was his.

He spent the night at the dwarf's house and regaled, with great humor, the day's events to Matilda, proudly confirmed by her smiling happy husband. In the morning he presented the consent-of-sale to Mrs. Chichester's agent in San Jose. Luck, as often, was with the intrepid Bobolo. The agent was already considering putting the Alviso property up for sale and, when Bobolo offered his two lots in San Francisco in straight exchange, clearly more valuable in the agent's eyes than the "ark property," the agent leaped at the opportunity without further discussion and they closed the deal. *"Buona Fortuna"* in the twinkling of a brief weekend had made Bobolo a happy man and had swung his future in an entirely new direction.

Bobolo returned home by train, wondering how he should present the weekend's events to his little flame. Despite the atmosphere which was charged with negative electricity because he was fourteen hours overdue, Bobolo walked confidently and open-heartedly into the anticipated buzz saw.

"Fiammella mine, good hunting and good news. Very good news!"

"And what may the good news be?" she asked dully without looking up from a soapy washbasin. "Is it good news that you're a day late and that there are fifty things for you to do around the house and our property? To be good enough, it would have to be news that you'd inherited a million lire!"

"We've come into possession of more than that, my good Fiammella, more than that."

"Millantatore (Exaggerator)!" Fiammella turned on him, withdrew her soapy hands from the basin in which she was scrubbing the children's clothes, and pushed the knuckles down on her hips in a say-that-again-and-mean-it posture.

Bobolo bravely inched forward. "We now, my dear wife, own a hilltop in Alviso with a view worth more than a million lire! We're moving there bag and baggage as soon as possible. We are moving back to Tuscany. Wait until you see the location and the views. The only missing item is the Arno."

"Is that so, my happy husband! And with whose and what money did you buy a crazy hilltop in Alviso?"

"I sold our two lots here."

Fiammella was stunned, unable to move. "No! No! No!" Her voice rose to a high pitch. Their two lots in San Francisco?

"Yes, yes, yes."

"You stupid, wild, insane man! Don't you know how valuable our San Francisco lots are, even after the earthquake? And how do you expect to make a living out there in the howling wilderness?"

"We'll open a country inn."

"Is that so? And how many people would traipse out there to take rooms in a backwoods wilderness or eat on a God-forsaken hilltop?"

"Plenty. You'll see. It's as beautiful as our Tuscany. And such a fine healthy life for the children away from so many people and so much cold fog. The location is outstanding; it's a wonderful area for children to roam free and get a feeling for the beauty of nature. We'll raise our own vegetables, plant grapes for our own *vino*. You'll fall in love with the place, Fiammella. It's Heaven on Earth."

"Ah, *demonio*, it's more likely Hell … and being married to you is often Hell!"

In her displeasure, Fiammella turned to the large soapy washbasin, picked it up and hurled its contents — foaming soapy water and wet clothes — at Bobolo. He became a dripping clothes-rack. Beatrice and Laura, who were standing at the kitchen door watching the verbal battle, ran way in laughter.

With quiet dignity, Bobolo wiped his eyes, picked off the sopping garments one by one with arched forefinger and thumb, dropped them to the floor and said, "Now you know why I sometimes come home late from work or hunting, Fiammella. It's always a pleasure to engage in such congenial discussions with you. We now have to complete our tasks up here because we will be leaving soon to establish our new home above San Jose. I understand why you are upset. People are uncomfortable with the unknown. I still confidently believe that you and the children will love it there, but regardless, the decision has been made."

The quarrel did not end there; it continued unabated for three days. Then cholera broke out in a section of San Francisco only eight blocks from their house. Bobolo's point about moving south was won without further argument.

The children never forgot the journey from San Francisco to Alviso in mid-May of 1906. It was a caravan. Because of Papa Bobolo, it was a joyous, singing event. There were three cart-loads of family possessions and provisions. Fiammella drove her horse-drawn cart at the rear, carrying the two youngest children, the wedding trunk, parcels and packets of clothing, the sewing machine, chairs and tables. Passerino drove the middle cart carrying more furniture and miscellaneous bundles. Bobolo drove the first horse-pulled cart, loaded with provisions and animals, sacks of flour and cereals, a barrel of molasses and one of olive oil, crates of wine, six crates of squawking Leghorn chickens, two cats, six rabbits, Beatrice, the oldest child, and Leo the dog.

Bobolo was in high spirits. He smacked the reins over the shoulders of Airone, the horse. Bobolo always had a reason for names. The Italian word *airone* means heron, a graceful flying bird. Beatrice was named for the beloved of Dante, Laura for Petrarch's lady. Bobolo himself had been named after the Boboli Gardens in Florence because he had been born in an apartment overlooking them.

Now Bobolo began to sing the jolly song *"Tiritomba"*:

> *Sera jette, sera jette a la marina,*
> *Pe trovà 'na 'namorata,*
> *Janca e rossa, janca e rossa aggraziata . . .*
> *Fatta proprio pe' scialà*
> *Tiritomba, tiritomba ...*

> One time in the evening, in the evening I went to the seaside,
> To find a girlfriend (for myself),
> Of light skin and rosy cheeks, of light skin, rosy cheeks and very graceful,
> With whom I can live my life in joyful fun.
> Tiritomba, tiritomba ...

The kids loved the song and always laughed when, as the two former lovers walked along the seashore, the papa accosted them, "flourishing his cane with language quite atrocious —*"Tiritomba, tiritomba ... !"*

Bobolo sang Italian operatic airs and Italian nursery songs. He told stories and he laughed a great deal, an infectious laugh his children loved. He described the life of gypsies and said that they were all going to be as free and happy as gypsies for the rest of their days. They made their meals by the roadside. Bobolo and Passerino brought out their guitars and sang to the limit of their joy and their lungs. The children danced and sang and romped around them. Even Fiammella seemed to cheer up a bit and to forget her resentment over the loss of their home in San Francisco. It was the jolliest caravan on the route between the city of St. Francis and the city of St. Joseph since Spanish days.

When the sky was the color of ripe lemons just after sunset of the second day, the caravan arrived at the summit of the hill-plateau of Alviso. The valley was gilded green, the distant hills like the purple iris on the banks of the Arno.

"Isn't it beautiful?" cried Bobolo, stretching out his arms with fervor, as if he owned the entire landscape.

Fiammella took in the scene from the practical standpoint. "Beautiful, yes. But to live here? No. *Impossible.* Imprudent man. *Imprudentissimo!*"

"Nothing is impossible, my dear. Come, let's put up our tents."

The next morning, in his happy excitement, Bobolo unpacked everything, even the furniture for which there was as yet no house. He set out chairs, tables, sofa, as if in imaginary rooms. The trunk and the sewing machine had places of honor. He let loose the Leghorn chickens, the dog, the cats and every animal except the rabbits. The hill was like a zoo run wild. He unpacked all the provisions.

In his nervous happy hurry, Bobolo dropped two bottles of wine which bounced but did not shatter on the hillside. However, when he un-roped the barrel of molasses and it fell from the cart to the ground, the barrel split open, molasses slowly oozing out, flowing like a river of sticky lava. It overtook several unwary chickens, engulfing them by their feet. The Leghorns pulled their gummy feet and looked very surprised when they got nowhere, proceeding in slow-motion, as if in a nightmare. Bobolo and Passerino erupted in laughter but Fiammella didn't see the humor at all. She knelt down, gave up trying to free the feet of the chickens and then concentrated on trying to save a few ladles of molasses. Bobolo and Pio turned away, suppressing laughter into unobtrusive smiles.

Fiammella muttered to herself until she gave up trying to save the molasses. Then began her tirade. "Laughing as our staples flow over the hillside, making it uninhabitable. Laughing as we turn into nomadic gypsies. What a fool I married. What an imbecile ..." Both men failed to contain their raucous laughter.

On the second day, Bobolo made an enclosure for the chickens, smiling and singing. Water had to be brought from a well a quarter of a mile away. Fiammella neither sang nor smiled, her face set in a scowl.

On the third day, Passerino went back to town with the one borrowed horse and cart. His own he would pick up later. The family Bonomo was alone on their hilltop. Bobolo got out his shovel, put it over his shoulder and started walking away. Fiammella immediately asked, "Where are you going now, madman?"

"To find the best place to start digging a well. That will also help tell us the best place to situate our house and our inn."

"Well, at least we agree on that," said Fiammella. "What will you do next?"

"You should remember that the Good Book tells us that the first thing the great Noah did was to plant a vineyard. After I dig the well, I am planting a vineyard."

As Fiammella walked rapidly back to the tents, she visualized through her tears the whole hill flowing with squandered wine and molasses. How can we ever survive in this isolated wasteland? Why did I ever decide to get married and come to the United

States with this impractical man? A vineyard should be far down the list of our priorities!

It was clear that, whatever she wanted or said, she was just whistling in the wind. If Bobolo wanted to plant a vineyard, over a thousand logical reasons *not* to do so, Bobolo would start his vineyard. He is indeed the devil in disguise. I wish he had remained in Crete and that I had disappeared into the real Tuscan hills to continue my happy, unrestrained single life.

Chapter 4

AMBULATORY FLAG

By the time school opened in early September, Bobolo Bonomo had a fine house. By shrewdly inviting Italian friends down from San Francisco for several days at a time for outdoor living, feasting, a bit of hunting and much working, he had managed to borrow enough of their time and labor to raise his house at minimal cost. Now and then professional assistance had been necessary from some of Mrs. Chichester's carpenters. Under Bobolo's supervision, the house had, of course, been built to the sound of hammers, saws, song and laughter.

Bobolo would have liked a stone house similar to structures built for centuries in his beloved Tuscany but the cost of stone was too high. For the present, a wooden house painted white with deep violet trim which brought back memories of the Mediterranean Basin would have to suffice. He had plans to transform the inn into stone and brick in the future, and to import Italian cypress trees to add to the Tuscan flavor of his property. He told Fiammella that one day he would paint a great fresco of garlands of purple grapes all around the house. She raised the broom to swat him but he ducked and dodged in time. His greatest athletic agilities had been honed in just such domestic escapes.

"You and your grapes!" she shouted. "You and your fancy ideas! Anything to avoid real work!"

"A few satyrs and nymphs, peeping among the grape leaves ...
Ah, there's an idea, *cara mia*. What a house! It shall be the happiest
house in California! In all America!"

"I'm sure you'd paint a strip of naked women clear around the
house if you could!"

"A colossal idea, *mia cara*." And off he went, dodging the
broom again.

If only it *could* be the happiest house. Left to Bobolo alone, it
would be, *certamente*, he said to himself, but Fiammella, nervous-
as-a-wasp Fiammella, took things so hard. She had nothing
remotely resembling a light touch towards the great opportunities
presented by life. She saw life as *au tragique* instead of *au comique*.

Bobolo shrugged and went off to the Chamber of Mirth that
he had made for himself on the ground floor of one of the three
guest houses, the one farthest from the main house. This guest
house was reserved for cronies of Bobolo, mainly males but not
entirely. Suitable congenial ladies who loved to laugh, always
accompanied by their spouses, were also allowed. This house
was twenty-five yards from the nearest other guest house because
Bobolo, with his keen understanding of human nature, predicted
that the combination of jokes, laughter and grapes *might* lead to a
somewhat greater amount of clamor from time to time. The other
two guest houses would be under Fiammella's jurisdiction. Not
this one, *per Bacco!*

The walls of his special room, his own cheerful, happy room,
were painted in bright horizontal stripes a foot wide in the red,
green and white flag colors of his beloved Italy. An American
flag stood in a bracket beside the entrance door. On the walls
were hung Bobolo's school certificates and the parchment stating
that he had successfully completed two years at the University of
Florence. Over the fireplace were the red hat he had worn and the
rifle he had used in the Greco-Turkish campaign of 1897 as well
as his hunting rifles and shotguns. To the side of the mantle were
lithographs of Tuscan scenes and a fine colored copy of the Giotto
portrait of Dante. A bookcase on the other side of the mantel

held such Italian classics as Dante's *Divine Comedy*, Boccaccio's *Decameron*, Tasso's *Gerusalemme Liberata*, Garibaldi's *Spedizione dei Mille* and Massimo D'Azeglio's *Ettore Fieramosca*, all of which Bobolo had not only read but had studied as a student.

A table in a corner held decanters of wine, bottles of brandy and rum, boxes of honey candies called *torroni,* canisters of coffee, glasses, siphons and funnels. Pushing out from one corner of the house was an ample restaurant-type kitchen with a modern stove where Bobolo made his happy mixture of rum and coffee or cooked special meals for friends or for himself alone when an angry, temperamental Fiammella exiled him from the main house.

In the opposite corner, a door led down to Bobolo's ample cool wine cellar, including barrels of wine being mellowed. In the center of the room was a table covered with red-checked oilcloth, cafe style, with six simple chairs set around it. Happiness did not depend upon luxury.

In the low ceiling over the chair at the head of the table, Bobolo, the irrepressible, who could never resist the *beffe* or buffooneries of the true Tuscan, had installed a sprinkler concealed in a small rose-glass chandelier, operable from a wire and button under his own chair. Under other chairs, small water pipes, barely visible where their spouts emerged over the chair corners, were set to wet the trousers of guests who misbehaved and were not yet initiated into Bobolo's Secret Order of Pranks. It was a room for eating, drinking, laughing and making merry — a room of mirth — suitably far away from the main house.

In the basement of the main house was the pastry-kitchen where Bobolo occasionally helped his wife turn out her excellent breakfast delights and desserts until he might be chased out by oven shovel or broom.

On the hill slopes, Bobolo planted not only his vineyard but a small orchard of cherries, plums, peaches and various citrus fruits. With help from his Italian friends, Bobolo had also started a vegetable garden from which large cabbages became his prize product. This one acre area was protected by a low wire fence. The white Leghorn chickens, now numbering two hundred, wandered freely over the hillside but not in the vegetable garden.

By now, of course, Bobolo knew almost everyone within a radius of several miles. Not only had he called on them to explain what he was planning for his property but he had also taken little presents to them, such as vegetables as they became available. There were several neighboring Italian families, a Spanish family, Señora Morello and her son, on the next slope, and assorted Americans down the hill and in the village. Whatever their national origins, his neighbors were friendly, more so when they came to know Bobolo and his happy sense of humor.

Bobolo had begun to supervise the building of Lady Chichester's ark, doing much of the simpler work himself, always getting approval in advance from her. He lifted the ark eight feet off the ground on a cement pedestal shaped like the original ark of Noah and painted it blue. Above the rows of real windows he painted rows of artificial windows with brilliantly colored animals leaning out of these windows in grotesque postures and with ludicrously smiling faces. On top of the lightning rod, a white dove floated with its message of "All aboard!" People began to drive past the property to take a look, and the Bonomo hospitality business at the new Bonomo Country Inn began to thrive despite Fiammella's pessimistic predictions. She turned out to be an excellent innkeeper, a fine Italian chef and baker. In time, Fiammella became known not just as the wife of Bobolo, but as the well-liked, capable hostess of the Bonomo Country Inn. Bobolo was proud of her, though she continued her not-infrequent denunciations of him.

Beatrice age nine, Laura age seven, and Tranquillino age five walked happily down the hill to their first day of school in the village in September 1907, one and a half years after the San Francisco earthquake.

Bobolo was at work hoeing weeds in his cabbage patch when his children returned from school. He tended to work moderately hard but never overly hard. It just wasn't his style. He accomplished a great deal but took frequent breathers, leaning on his hoe, his hands curved over the staff's end, his chin resting on his hands, taking in the atmosphere and often doing important thinking. He looked down at his big green cabbages, the pride of his vegetable garden, and was reminded of the large cabbages the newly-retired Roman Emperor Diocletian so proudly began growing in 305 AD in the gardens of his retirement palace in Dalmatia, now the city of Split in Croatia.

Bobolo was content. This was his new life — designed, created and lived at his own happy speed. While Bobolo was day-dreaming, still leaning on his hoe, the children came running up the hill to the cabbage patch. The two girls were wailing at the tops of their out-of-breath lungs while young Tranquillino loitered behind to watch with manly restraint.

Beatrice, the leader of the pack, reached her father first. "Oh Papa, we don't want to go to school any more, ever, ever!"

Bobolo dropped his hoe on the ground and leaned down to the unhappy child. She threw her arms around his neck and proclaimed though wild sobs, "Oh Papa, Papa! They called us 'Little Dago' and 'Woppie, Woppie'! They pulled my pigtails and, oh, it hurt so much! I thought my pigtails would come out of my head and pull out my brains! But what they said hurt much more. They told me to tell my Papa to take us back where we came from, to Italy! They don't want any more *dagoes* at their school. Tranquillino fought, too. Come here, Tranquillino, and show Papa your nose and the bruises on your arms. Laura didn't get hurt because she ran into the school building and hid in the toilet. Oh, Papa, I want to be American like the rest of them. I don't want to be Italian. Why do I have to be an Italian, Papa?"

Bobolo took his arms from around the child and stood up from his kneeling position. "Never let me hear you say that again, Beatrice. Never. You're nine years old and should know better. Come with me, all of you, to my *rifugio* (refuge) … I have things to say to you — very important things." He briefly examined Tranquillino's nose and arms, found no fractured bones sticking out and reassured him that his minor wounds would heal quickly.

He pushed open the door of his Chamber of Mirth and sat the children around the oilcloth covered table. He took a handful of *torroni* from the jar and placed them down on the table in front of his children, as the dramatic sobs dwindled.

"Now listen to me," Bobolo said in a firm but quiet voice. "You were born in America. You are American just as much as your classmates. I was born in Italy but I am almost American, too. What do you think I've been studying for during the last two years? To take out my American citizenship papers! It is wonderful to be an American, as I soon hope to be. But I am as yet still Italian and so is Mama. And you are Italian *by origin* and that is a great thing! *Never forget that!* Your grandparents were Italian and all of your ancestors back to the glorious days of the Roman Empire. It is magnificent to be Italian — magnificent, I say!

"Julius Caesar and Augustus Caesar and Marcus Aurelius were Italian — you will study about them in school. Cato and Cicero were Italian, and the great Dante Alighieri. Beatrice, you are named for his beloved sweetheart whom he made immortal with his poetry. And Francesco Petrarch, for whose dear Laura you were named, Laura, was another immortal Italian poet. And Christopher Columbus, who discovered America, was Italian. Tell your schoolmates that! And tell them that Italy had been great for two thousand years before America was even discovered. We love liberty here but we didn't *invent* liberty. Long before Thomas Jefferson and the makers of the Declaration of Independence there were those who fought for liberty of body and spirit in Italy. And afterwards, in our time, there were the great liberators from tyranny, the men of freedom, Mazzini and Cavour and Garibaldi. What I'm trying to tell you is that Italy was civilized two thousand years before America even existed. Do you hear that? Your schoolmates are barbarians if they don't know that. Do you understand?"

"Yes, Papa," they said. "Yes, Papa."

"Well, then, never let anyone make fun of Italy, *Italia superba, gloriosa, illustrissima* — proud and glorious and illustrious Italy."

"But how can I make a speech about Italy when somebody's pulling my pigtails?" asked Dante's sweetheart.

"Beat the stuffing out of anyone who speaks ill of Italy or Italians or calls you names. When they're down wriggling in the dust, then tell them about Italy. Shout it so that everyone can hear! Beat the cussedness out of anyone who ever calls you *dagoes* or wops, for they mean no good by it. Of course *dago* once meant simply a person called Diego and wop meant *guappo*, a conceited Spanish man. But now these words express contempt. They really mean 'Hate the Italians. Down with the Italians; we are better than Italians.' This kind of bad talk is not acceptable in America. And if someone doesn't know that, *you* will be the one to teach him!"

"Well, Beatrice can go back to school, Papa, but I can never go back," whimpered Laura. "Beatrice and Tranquillino know how to fight but I don't know how, Papa."

"Laugh it off, then, Laura. Laughter's as good a weapon as any other and often better. Laughter's a shining sword made of rays of light. You can win lots of arguments and fights with laughter."

"Is that why you laugh so much, Papa?"

"That is Bobolo's secret, little one. I'm not telling."

"But if the children still tease?" asked Laura.

"If they still tease, come back and tell me and I'll go talk to the school principal. But by Bacchus, I feel like running up the Italian flag from the top of our house to show the world we're not ashamed of Italy! By God, I think I will! I'm proud of Italy! I'll show them!"

Beatrice began to sob again. "Oh, Papa, please promise us you won't do that. Things are bad enough now. We'd be the laughing stock of the whole world! Please promise us!" She took his hand and squeezed it. Before her papa could promise, Mama appeared in the doorway.

"What goes on here? What is this, the Great *Consiglio di Stato* (Council of State)? Get to your chores, children. And back to the cabbage patch with you, Papa! What are you doing, teaching them to forget their tasks and their duties? Turning them into little lazy good-for-nothings, like yourself? Out with you! All of you!"

"On the contrary, Fiammella. I'm teaching them their duty."

"Set a good example, then. Wagging your tongue at them won't make them better children."

Papa let out a laugh.

"See," said Beatrice to Laura as they left the room, arms around each other. "See how Papa uses a laugh to win an argument?"

The next day, as the imp of fortune arranged it, or rather as Bobolo arranged it for he himself made the suggestion, Fiammella went to San Jose to do some fall shopping for the children. That gave Bobolo a free field for his operations. During the night, since the children clearly did not approve of flying the Italian flag from the roof-top, he dreamed up an alternative ploy to proclaim the glory of Italy.

The second day at school went better for the children than the first. The fists of Beatrice and Tranquillino convinced a number of bullying schoolmates that perhaps it would be better not to meddle with this clan. Several of the Fontana and Petri children, whose Italian families were already affluent from their wineries, came to the pugilistic support of the battling Bonomos. Laura's little smile even gained some friends.

So it was that on this second happier afternoon of homecoming from school that Beatrice, Laura and Tranquillino arrived swinging their strapped books, talking and laughing up the hill. No sobs, no tears. But, when they came in view of their home slope, they stopped, paralyzed with horror. Papa, oh Papa, how *could* you?

Their father had carried out his threat to proclaim to the world the glory of Italy. Would that he had run up the Italian flag on the roof-top instead! How correctible *that* would have been! But their father had taken one-third of the two hundred white Leghorn chickens and dipped them in basins of bright green paint. He had taken another third and dipped them in bright scarlet paint. The final third remained in their pristine whiteness.

As two hundred fowl ranged all over their property in plain sight of all passersby, the painted Leghorns created the unmistakable massed colors of the flag of Italy — red, green and white.

"PAPA! How could you?" lamented Beatrice, when they found Papa in the garden. Tranquillino, similar in personality to Bobolo, laughed in approbation of his unpredictable, amazing father.

"Give a salute, I say," replied Papa. "Give two salutes — first to the American flag on the gatepost and then to the glorious ambulatory flag of Italy scattered all over our hills!"

Chapter 5

THE GHOST

Bobolo's refuge room, his Chamber of Mirth, became more and more a gathering place for convivial Italians living either in San Francisco or the southern part of the Bay Area. Pio Passerino came by train twice a month from his apartment in San Francisco. On a Saturday night one could be sure to find in Bobolo's guest house such steady frequenters as Tito Ruggero (Lady Chichester's chef), Merlo, his hunter friend from San Jose, Angelo Bellucci, the ruggedly handsome Head of the Catholic Novitiate a mile away, and Serafino Pipitone, the amusing garage mechanic, amateur inventor and gifted cornet player, full of surprises and laughter but occasionally a bit quick-tempered after excessive absorption of *vino*.

Sometimes the Italian priest, Father Simeoni, dropped in for some intellectual and religious sparring with Bobolo and "just to taste" Bobolo's food and wine. The budding wine tycoons from the Petri and Fontana families might drop by for a convivial meal, conversation and light-hearted laughter. Sandro would also frequently join the Saturday afternoon and evening gatherings. He was the jack-of-all-trades whom Bobolo had hired as handyman despite Fiammella's protests of runaway costs, to help reduce the always-lengthy "To Do" list of his unrelenting wife.

Sandro only attended these jolly social gatherings about once a month, sat at the dinner table or in a corner, smiling pleasantly but rarely talking. He gave up school after the sixth grade because he didn't like it and didn't do well. He learned many skills and crafts from his father, an accomplished tradesman. Because of the group's always-angelic behavior, the Saturday Night Group called themselves "The Angels Club" or "The Angels," for short. They usually didn't disband until Sunday afternoon, sleeping in guest houses on Saturday night, particularly the one containing the Chamber of Mirth, which had extra beds, on Saturday nights.

One afternoon in October of Bobolo's second year on the hill, Sandro was absent and Serafino was late to arrive. It was Columbus Day and Bobolo had given Sandro the day off so he could spend it in San Francisco, where he had never been in his life.

Brought up on a ranch south of San Jose, being shy and not good in school, he remained on the ranch most of the time. As his brothers got older, it was they who accompanied their father on marketing trips to San Jose and San Francisco to sell their cherries, walnuts, wine and olives.

Early this morning Bobolo had put Sandro on the train for San Francisco, had told him how to get to Columbus Square for the big parade, speeches, mass at St. Mary's Church and the general Columbus Day celebration. He had also put a ticket to the Alcazar Theater in Sandro's pocket and had told him in English to go to the theater "to see the best stock show in the city." Shadowy figures of prize cows and steers had risen in Sandro's mind at the word "stock."

Bobolo gave some extra spending money to Sandro and said, "Make a long day of it, have a good time and take the midnight train back. *Addio*, Sandro."

It was obvious, therefore, why Sandro was absent from the group but it was a little alarming that Serafino was late, for he had been out on the hills mushroom hunting the previous Sunday and had insisted on putting into his leather pouch some pink-gilled mushrooms that Bobolo had declared poisonous. Serafino, however, had emphatically stated not only that they were safe but excellent for the health. There was no use arguing with Serafino.

Several years previously he had popped out an eye during the fervor of his cornet playing. When he became angry in any altercation, sometimes he would pluck out his glass eye and smash it against some solid object, an expensive and disconcerting display.

Bobolo had proved correct in his recognition of the poisonous mushrooms. Serafino had been deathly ill for days with confusion, obtundation and hallucinations but, under the treatment of Dr. Nollins, the best doctor in the village below the Bonomo Country Inn, he had recovered and gone back to work at the garage on the day previous.

"What if Pipitone relapsed and died?" remarked Tito, lifting a glass of sparkling burgundy, one of the beverages with which Bobolo was honoring Columbus Day.

"Ah, he would be a poor ghost," sighed Angelo Bellucci. "One could well write a poem about *The Silent Bombardino* (cornet player)."

"Poor soul, rather," said Passerino, "for, of course, in Catholic theology there are only living souls and souls in transition. No ghosts. I fear Serafino will have a long eternity in Purgatory because of his cynical non-beliefs."

"He'll have good company if he goes to Purgatory," commented Bobolo, "for there and in Hell are all the truly merry souls! Listen — I think I hear his wagon clattering up the hill. *Eureka!* I have an idea. A stupendous idea! When he comes in, let's continue to talk as we've been talking. Let's pretend not to see him, not to know he is in the room. He will soon think he *is* a ghost! Promise me, my friends. Promise me! It will be the best practical joke we've ever played. Don't see him. Don't hear him."

Tito and Angelo slapped their haunches with glee. Passerino looked dubious.

"You're with us, Little Sparrow? You won't spoil it?" asked Bobolo.

"Very well. It's a good trick. But — *povero Serafino* (poor Serafino)!" They shook hands, all of them. Then Bobolo hastily took Serafino's customary chair and the only extra chair and

shoved them through the corner door into the wine cellar. Tito
and Angelo moved their chairs into the center of their sides of the
table, Passerino occupying, as usual, the place opposite Bobolo.
There was now no place left for Serafino.

It was only a moment before Serafino, looking very pale,
appeared in the doorway. The silver cornet under his arm gleamed
in the light of the rose chandelier. Serafino was a figure cut on a
somewhat skewed pattern by some celestial comedian. His mouth
went up a little slantwise towards his left ear. That ear jutted out
from his head while the right ear remained clamped close to his
skull. His left eyebrow matched the upward slant of his mouth.
The eyebrows were straw-colored, while his hair was brown. His
eyes, the real one and the false, were pale greenish blue.

"*Buona sera. Buona sera, amici* (Good evening, friends),"
greeted Serafino, expecting an extra-special welcome this evening
after his bout with death.

No one looked towards the door. Bobolo, as if continuing
a conversation, said, "And I'm sure that when the good angels
hear Serafino playing his cornet for them, they'll put aside their
harps and say, 'Harps, go your ways. Cornets shall now be the
instruments of Heaven!'"

"Too bad, too bad. *Povero* Serafino. To die so young! Poor
Serafino," murmured Tito Ruggero, leaning his head far back to
take a big quaff of sparkling burgundy.

"What do you mean, 'Too bad, *povero* Serafino,' and talking
about angels and death and all the rest?" asked the *bombardino*,
bringing himself and his cornet inside the door. Nobody looked up.

"Aren't you fellows getting hungry?" asked Bobolo. "If Beatrice
doesn't bring in our spaghetti — and tonight it's *Spaghetti alle
Vongole* (Spaghetti with Clams) — in exactly three minutes I'll go
get it myself or pull her in by the hair. Too bad, it was one of our
dear departed's favorite recipes. Remember how Serafino loved it?"

Serafino set his cornet against the wall and came to the table.
"Where's my chair? I'm tired of this silly conversation," he said
firmly. Nobody paid any attention.

"You're not that kind of a papa, Bobolo," said Angelo. "I can't see you pulling Beatrice in by the hair."

"As for Fiammella, that's a different matter," added Passerino with a wink. Everyone laughed except Serafino.

"Ah yes," remarked Bobolo. "Anyone who says 'woman' means 'woe-man!'"

"What's the matter with you *imbecilli?*" shouted Serafino. "I'm *here*. Where's my chair?"

"But Serafino's wife," declared Bobolo, "showed herself to be a good woman, a truly devoted wife at the funeral yesterday. I wish I could think that *my* wife would weep so much for me at *my* funeral! How that woman wept bitterly for our Serafino! Enough to fill a swimming pool! She really loved him."

"What's this? What are you *imbecilli* saying? Do you think I'm *dead?*" ranted Serafino. "Look at me! Here I am alive, alive — Serafino Pipitone." His own hands searched his own body rather frantically, running up and down it. "Feel me! Touch me!" he urged his friends. He stretched out his arms over the table, his hands trembling.

No one moved a finger towards him.

"He was a good man," remarked Bobolo solemnly. "*Requiescat in pace* (Rest in peace). I wonder if he will be a happy ghost in Purgatory."

"Yes, he was a good man," supplemented Angelo. "A little nonsensical in some of his inventions … and a little high-tempered sometimes. I wonder how many glass eyes he's shattered since he lost his actual eye."

"And unrepentant for his sins, poor fellow," added Passerino, "for which he will serve many eons of pain and torture in Purgatory and Hell. *Povero* Serafino …"

"But a *buonamima* (dear departed) just the same, a good fellow," added Bobolo. "I'll drink to his ghost."

"A thousand devils! Don't you see me?" exclaimed Serafino. He leaned over and pushed Bobolo on the forehead. Bobolo showed himself an excellent actor when playing for laughs; he gave only the briefest of blinks and went right on talking. "It must be interesting to be a discarnate soul, a ghost wandering the earth, able to see everything and everybody, and, of course, he would still have only one eye. In a way, strolling around and seeing but not being seen might be fun."

"Fun?" exclaimed Serafino, and for the first time he began to wonder whether he was really now a ghost. Almighty God! Had he really died and been buried yesterday? He'd been dreadfully ill with fever and bad dreams and suffering but he thought he'd gotten well and had risen from his bed still on earth. Could he really have passaged silently down into Purgatory instead? He felt himself all over again while his friends watched out of the corners of their eyes, trying their best not to smile. He felt his left arm with his right hand, then his right arm with his left hand. Then he ran both hands over his face. He *seemed* solid and real enough, but perhaps that was the delusory essence of ghosts … they felt real only to *themselves.* He began to tremble all over but he made one last desperate effort. He pounded Passerino on the back while Passerino did his best to keep an unpounded expression on his face.

"Passerino! Passerino! Don't you see me, Little Sparrow? You're an honest man — not like Bobolo, the trickster, the *buffone.* Little Sparrow, you see me, don't you?"

Passerino was moved and felt pity. But Bobolo, reaching his hand under the table, quietly opened the gauge controlling Passerino's chair and deluged his hind side with cold water. Passerino buried his expression of dismay by taking a big gulp of wine.

"Angelo! Angelo! *Amico mio.* For the love of God, you see me, don't you? Say you see me!" cried Serafino, stretching out both of his hands to Belluccio.

With a swift but subtle gesture, Bobolo also flooded Angelo's chair. Angelo stiffened as he took a quick mouthful of *vino* and said, "This is damned good wine!"

"Ah, but wait until you taste next year's wine from my own good vines! That will be the best wine ever made, *per Bacco*. Better than Petri's, better than Fontana's," declared Bobolo.

"Here's to Bacchus — and Bobolo!" toasted Tito, the only one feeling guilty about Serafino's suffering. Tito and the others lifted their glasses.

"Tito, good Tito — you see me, I'm sure of it! You see me, I'm here!"

"Here's to a long life for the remaining four of us!" toasted Bobolo.

"Yes, here's to a long and fruitful life to the four of us," cried the Angelic conspirators loudly.

"And to the ghost of poor Serafino," added Bobolo in a stentorian voice.

"Yes, to the ghost of poor Serafino," assented the other three.

Serafino let out a wild, distraught yell and, plucking his glass eye from its socket, threw it against the pink chandelier which smashed in rose-petal shards all over the table. Still screaming, Serafino fled the room, leaving his glass eye rolling on the table and his cornet leaning against the wall. He dashed outside, bumping headlong into Beatrice, knocking the platter of *spaghetti alle vongole* out of her hands onto the dirt of the yard.

"My goodness! What in heaven's name has happened to Pipitone?" asked a distressed Beatrice from the open door. "Did you see what he just did?"

"Pipitone? Pipitone? What are you talking about? Pipitone hasn't been here," answered Bobolo.

"Who was it, then, who knocked the platter of spaghetti from my hands, a ghost?"

"Yes, it must have been a ghost!" And everyone in the room erupted loudly.

"Well, then, here's another ghost," said Beatrice. "Here's Sandro back from the city. I'll clean up the mess and bring you another platter — if Mama lets me. Won't she be mad about her broken platter and all those wasted clams and spaghetti? I'd still like to know what you jokesters did to Pipitone."

"We didn't do anything bad. Did you know, my child, that people like to have something done to them. Something is always better than nothing. Remember that. It's a whole philosophy of life. Attention to someone means affection, and *vice versa*."

"Oh, Papa!" lamented Beatrice, sounding a bit like her mother. She stooped to pick up fallen globs of spaghetti and the largest fragment of broken china. She was blocking the entrance of Sandro who now stood in the open doorway.

"Why, Sandro! What happened?! I told you to go to the play and come back on the midnight train and yet here you are back at ten o'clock. Didn't you go to the play?"

"Well, Signor Bobolo," he replied in his slow, humorless voice. "I went to that place where you said there would be a stock show. They took my ticket all right and then a pretty girl took me to a room with a kind of platform in it and set me down in a front seat. Pretty soon some people came out on the platform and began to discuss their love affairs in loud voices. I had no right to listen to all that talk about their private lives. I mayn't be no gentleman but I do know some things what isn't proper. It wasn't no place for me. I was expecting to see cattle at a stock show! So I come away early, that's all."

The Angels burst into laughter over Sandro's reaction to the theater. Bobolo, between gusts of laughter, tried to explain to Sandro about the game of pretending in theater performances, when another voice interrupted.

"Play-acting! Games! Fun! Laughing! Belly busting! Never a serious moment." The torrent came from the usual source, the perturbed mouth of Fiammella who had shoved Sandro out of the doorway and now stood there herself. *"In boccha chiusa non c'entrano le mosche* (Flies can't get into a closed mouth)," she commented bitterly.

"Nor does food, my dear Little Flame," replied Bobolo. "Where's our spaghetti?"

"I came to find out why you need so much spaghetti tonight. Are you feeding an army? The Greek Army, perhaps?" Fiammella was without humor but sometimes her flashes of sarcasm showed evidence of her quick turn of mind. Bobolo deflected the sarcasm with a laugh, as was his habit.

"*Toccato* (Touched, as in fencing)! A palpable hit, my dear. We're especially hungry tonight because we've laughed a great deal. And laughter is good for the health and very good for the appetite. Laughter is the antipasto to a great meal such as you always prepare, my dear Fiammella. Mirth is the fine wine that should accompany the Meal of Life from the first course to the last."

Fiammella mumbled something in a bitter tone, not appreciating her spouse's philosophizing.

"Must I then have Beatrice bring you another platter? You will be the ruin of us." Beatrice had not betrayed the reason for the broken platter.

"A full platter, very full," suggested Bobolo.

"And what was wong with Serafino? What in the Holy Virgin's name did you do to him? He went screaming down the hill like a mad man!"

"He thought he saw a ghost." All of the Angels laughed.

As Fiammella growled something untranslatable, Bobolo spread out his hands in the Italian gesture of futility and, addressing his cronies of The Angels Club, said, "Ah, my friends, life is great theater. Life is great, period. We'll soon have a fine meal to put in our bellies. *A tavola non s'invecchia* (At table one doesn't grow old). At one's own table and at The Great Table of Life, if one keeps a merry stomach and a merry heart, one truly never needs to grow old or to die prematurely like poor Pipitone!" Then Bobolo launched into Figaro's merry song, "*Figaro qui, Figaro qua!*"

Fiammella turned around and shouted through the door before departing for the kitchen:

"Bobolo qui, Bobolo qua!
Bobolo sempre niente fa!"

(Bobolo here, Bobolo there.
Bobolo always does nothing!)

Bobolo laughed, as was his benevolent approach to taming his shrew, a tactic which, so far in thirteen years of marriage, didn't seem to be working very well. His co-members of The Angels Club laughed with him … but several of them also had sympathetic expressions on their faces.

Chapter 6

UDDER PEACE

"Hey! Hey, you wicked beast! *Ti porti il diavolo* (The devil take you)! Swoosh! Off my property!" cried Bobolo loudly, flinging his hand at the errant cow. "I will shoot you dead, *morto*!"

The cow wagged her head nonchalantly and flicked her tail in a devil-may-care manner, then mooed loudly. The nearby remaining painted chickens squawked and scattered.

"No, no you won't, assassin. No shooting around here!" shouted Fiammella.

"But this is impossible. She is eating my precious prize cabbages again, the jewels of my garden. I must go over and lay down the law once to Señora Morello and tell her that the next time her naughty Clementina sneaks over the wire into my cabbage patch, I will indeed assassinate her with my shotgun."

"You'll shoot down who, the señora or the *vacca* (cow)?"

"La vacca! La vacca criminale! La vacca stupida!"

"The señora means no harm," said Fiammella. "I feel sorry for her. What a come-down! Her grandfather, the Spanish cattle rancher, owned all these hills and huge herds of cattle."

"Yes. I agree. She's a fine woman of noble lineage, but her cow did not inherit her good judgment. I think her cow is bewitched."

"I thought you didn't believe in bewitching, Bobolo. Why don't you hang some red flannel or red ribbon along your fence, as they do in Tuscany, to keep out the devil and all his works?"

"Superstitions! Folk magic! Old as the Etruscans, probably older. No, I'll shoot to kill. That's simpler and quicker."

Just before the children came home from school, Clementina got in again! She was in the patch calmly chewing cabbages as if she had been given Bobolo's personal invitation to dinner. Bobolo was nearing the boiling point.

He took hold of Beatrice as soon as she entered the yard. "Look here, Beatrice, I want you to do me a favor. I want you to run down immediately to the house of his Honor, the Judge, and get a license from him allowing me to shoot that infernal cow, Clementina, who is eating up all my beautiful cabbages."

"But, Papa ..."

"No 'but Papas!' I need help and you are my oldest child."

"But where does he live? How should I know where he lives?"

"As soon as you get to the village, just ask someone. Everyone will know where he lives. Be off. I hear he's a very nice man. Maybe he will give you a cookie." He gave her an affectionate pinch on her ear, turned her around gently in the direction of the village, then gave her a soft push to start her off.

What next, Beatrice wondered. How embarrassing. But my father does do lots of nice things for me. Beatrice adored her laughing father even though sometimes he had strange ideas! Like the painting of the chickens. People came from miles around to see the painted chickens and now so many people know all about our restaurant, Bonomo Country Inn and the guest houses. He even made an enormous sign to hang over the gate: PAINTED CHICKEN PARADISE. BEST ITALIAN FOOD IN AMERICA. The painted chickens were mostly gone now into the pot and Papa decided not to paint any more. The restaurant has been much more crowded since then, so maybe he's not so dumb after all. The Ark with its brightly-colored animals was also a drawing card, and Mama's excellent cooking was an even better attraction. Fiammella worked very hard in the kitchen. Bonomo Country Inn and its restaurant were prospering.

For a time, after the chicken episode, the children at school had had a field-day in the presence of the Bonomo youngsters, flapping their arms, clucking and going into gusts of laughter. That passed. Now Beatrice was sure that the story of the cow would spread through the village. She could already hear the children mooing.

It took all of Beatrice's courage to proceed down the hill. She didn't look right or left and didn't say anything to any children she saw along the way, especially in her age group. When she got to the village, she asked one lady on the street where the judge lived, and she gave Beatrice easy directions. Beatrice was reluctant to just go up and knock on a stranger's door but finally she mustered up the courage to do so. She found the door-bell and rang it.

The door opened and a kind voice asked, "Well, what can I do for you, young lady?"

"Oh, I need to talk to the judge for just a couple of minutes. It's very important, at least to my papa. Are you the judge?"

"Yes, I am, and I have time to talk with you." The judge led her into the living-room and sat her down in a large stuffed chair next to the fireplace. He told her to wait there for a moment, disappeared into the kitchen, and brought her back two large cookies. He sat down in the opposite easy chair. He had a somewhat plump face with twinkling brown eyes and a pleasant smile. "What is your papa's name?"

"He's Bobolo Bonomo and this is about a cow."

"A cow?"

"Yes, sir, our neighbor's wayward cow."

"Don't tell me your papa has painted your neighbor's cow red, green and white!" The judge's laughter rolled out uninhibited. Beatrice sank deeper into the chair. The judge regretted his little joke. She was an attractive child with mahogany-colored hair, olive skin, serious brown eyes and a sweetly curved mouth. The judge reached out a paternally patting hand. "You didn't tell me *your* name."

"Beatrice. I'm named after Dante's Beatrice."

The judge was a little misty about Italian literature but he replied, "I see. Well, Beatrice, suppose you tell me your cow story. Tell me everything you want me to know. I'm very much interested."

"Yes, sir." She moved forward in her chair. "Well, sir, you see our neighbor, Señora Morello, has a cow, Clementina. And my papa has a fine vegetable garden — tomatoes, peppers, lettuce, peas, beans, onions, garlic, spices and cabbages. Especially cabbages, which grow very big. My father is very proud of those cabbages."

"I see. Yes, go on, Beatrice."

"Well, Señora Morello's cow gets into my papa's vegetable garden all the time, every day. It's driving him crazy. So my papa asked me to come to you for a license to shoot the cow, Mr. Judge."

Twinkles appeared on the sides of the judge's eyes but his voice was solemn. "Does your papa not have a fence around the vegetable patch?"

"Well, yes, he does but it's low, to keep out the chickens."

"Barbed wire?"

"No, plain wire. And Clementina is very smart and always very hungry. She easily steps over the wire to get at Papa's prize cabbages."

The judge couldn't help smiling. He then asked, "Do you have a cow too, to supply you with milk?"

"No, sir."

"Where do you get your milk, then?"

"We buy Clementina's milk from Señora Morello."

"Well, well, well. And where, then, would your papa buy his milk if he shoots the bountiful supplier of his milk? That would be poor business, it seems to me. Very poor business indeed."

"I don't know, sir."

His logic made good sense. Beatrice sank back into the chair. How could Papa have sent her on such an embarrassing errand? The judge seems right and Papa seems wrong. "But my papa has worked so hard terracing that hill, planting his garden, dragging the water out to it, hoeing it, keeping all the nasty weeds out. How would you feel, Mr. Judge, if you'd made a wonderful garden and an intruder came and ate it all up? Wouldn't you feel like my papa does?"

"Wait a minute … the cow hasn't eaten all of your vegetables, has she?"

"No, sir. She seems to like just the big cabbages. And they're such beautiful cabbages."

"How many cabbages did she eat today?"

"About five."

"Well, cabbages are selling for about ten cents a head in the market today. You tell your father to go to his neighbor Mrs. Morello and ask her to pay him five times ten cents, which is fifty cents. That's all there is to it. See how simple that is? Your papa must arrange either to build a fence or to have Mrs. Morello tie up her cow. That's all."

"Then you can't give him a license? He'll be very angry with me if I don't bring him a license to shoot that cow. Very angry. He much prefers to laugh. He will be annoyed with you, too, Mr. Judge."

The judge spoke very emphatically now. "You tell your papa I'll be very angry with him if I hear of any harm to that hungry cow who doesn't know any better. Tell him that neighbors must live in peace. I am a Judge but also a Justice of the Peace. Remember to tell him that."

"Yes, sir."

"Tell him to relinquish the idea of a gun. Paint brushes are better than guns any day." The judge narrowed his eyes, vanquishing the twinkle. Beatrice felt uncomfortable as the judge went on. "Tell your papa that if he wants to sell me some of his cabbages before Clementina gets to them, I'll be glad to buy them."

"Thank you, sir." Beatrice went to the door sadly, feeling that she had failed in her mission. What seemed like good logic to the judge, and even to her, could set off an explosion in her Italian father.

Papa was waiting at the gate, gun in hand, ready to dispatch Clementina once and for all. He had even put on his red hunting cap and his leather hunting jacket. He was all primed, Beatrice realized, for one of his dramas. "Well, Beatrice? My license ... do you have it?"

"The judge didn't give me a license, Papa."

"*Dio mio* (Good God)! Isn't that his job, the damned old hog-bellied fool?"

"He didn't seem like a fool to me, Papa. He seemed like a kind, sensible man."

"Oh, he did, did he? I don't see anything sensible about him not giving me a license to shoot a criminal thieving cow!"

"I'll explain everything, Papa. Let's go into the house. Where's Mama?"

"In the kitchen."

"All right. Let's go there."

"No need stirring up Mama."

"Come on, Papa. I'll tell you both everything. The judge said some interesting things."

They went around into the kitchen where Mama was rolling out great layers of pasta for ravioli. The two other children were sitting on benches near the table, hoping for handouts of scraps. Sandro was there, too, since it was now getting too dark to work around the place. Since Mama still believed that Papa should do all the work on their property himself and that the hiring of Sandro was an unnecessary extravagance, she treated Sandro rather poorly. Sandro merely shrugged his shoulders, saying, in the language of shrugs, "*pazienza* (patience)." He was very devoted to Bobolo, who admired his handyman's craftsmanship and liked him as a person.

"Beatrice has been down to see the judge," announced Papa. "I sent her down for a license to shoot Clementina who eats my prize cabbages every day."

Mama brought down her rolling-pin hard on the pasta dough, as if on Bobolo's head. She rolled vehemently and the dough spread out quickly. Her cheeks were flushed and her teeth clenched but for the present she directed her emotions at the pasta and said nothing.

"Beatrice, tell us what the judge said," directed Bobolo.

"Well, the judge said, 'Where would your papa buy his milk if he shot the bountiful supplier of his milk? That would be poor business, it seems to me! Very poor business!'"

"He said that? Did he say nothing about the value of my beautiful cabbages? The solid gold of my prize cabbages?"

Mama banged the rolling pin and the pasta scrunched towards the edge of the table.

"He asked, 'How many cabbages did the cow eat today?' I told him 'about five.' 'Then,' said the judge, 'since cabbages are ten cents a head in the market today, all you have to do is to ask your neighbor, Mrs. Morello, to pay your papa fifty cents.'"

"*Birbone* (Rascal)! *Ladro* (Robber)! He said that? Ten cents a head for such magnificent cabbages? My cabbages are worth thousands of dollars to me, thousands of dollars!"

"*Scioccone* (Big fool)!" exclaimed Fiammella. "Great prince of merchants! We need milk much more than cabbages!"

Beatrice rushed on. "He said, too, 'Tell your papa that neighbors must live in peace and be nice to one another. If your papa wants to sell me some of his cabbages before Clementina eats them, I'll be glad to buy them.'"

"He said that?" queried Bobolo, raising his eyebrows. "*Un buon tipo* (a good sort), after all, the judge. He does his duty as he sees it."

"He also said, 'Tell him to go easy on the gun. Paint brushes are better than guns any day.' I almost died when he said that, Papa."

"Did he say it with a glint of a smile?"

"Yes, I think he did," she admitted. "But I don't think it was funny, Papa."

"Ah, a good man, the judge. He has a sense of humor."

Through the doorway there now came a strange sound. It was like the wailing of the wind through poplar trees in Tuscany in autumn. But this was a throated wailing.

In a moment Señora Morello appeared in the doorway clasping and unclasping her lifted hands and making the sound of ancient death lamentations. "Oh, Signor and Signora Bonomo. Woe is me! Woe is all of us. My blessed, blessed Clementina is dead. Dead! Never to give us good milk again."

"What happened?" asked Fiammella.

"An hour or so ago she took sick. Down on her haunches. Eyes rolled. Stomach puffed. Green foam at the mouth. So sad to see, so break my heart. I send Antonio for the vet. He come. He tell me she dead. He slit her up the stomach; he find green poison inside. Cabbages, she eat too many cabbages. Your cabbages, Signor. Clementina, my blessed cow. You kill her with your cabbages. You kill her. How I forgive? Oh, my Clementina, my Clementina!" she rocked and wailed.

A dramatic event, not of Bobolo's making, had presented itself full-blown. Often at his best in a crisis, Bobolo went forward to meet the occasion with a kind of majesty. He approached the bereaved señora, laid his hand tenderly upon her shoulder and said, "My dear, dear señora, your sorrow is our sorrow, *dal cuore*, to the uttermost depths of our hearts. Your cow was *our* cow, for the milk that she yielded has entered our bodies and is now flesh of our flesh, blood of our blood. She consumed our cabbages, yes. But our cabbages, alas, in the end consumed her. I will tell you what I will do, dear señora. Although no one could ever take blessed Clementina's place in our hearts, I will, on one condition, buy *half* of a new cow."

"Half? Of a new cow? How, Signor?"

"Yes, half. Is that not fair since we are both responsible for her death? I through my beloved cabbages; you for allowing your cow to frequently ravage my garden. I will contribute half the money to buy a new Clementina. I will own two swelling udders; you will be selling two udders."

"A cow, in half?" The poor señora's mind was befuddled.

"A whole cow to provide milk for our two families, dear Señora."

Fiammella cast a dark look at her husband from the counter where the ravioli were now reposing in perfectly even ribbons. Bobolo was behaving so gallantly, so tenderly. What had come over him? Who really slaved for the money that he so lightly proffered? Then it occurred to her that it was a shrewd bargain he was driving. If he paid for half the cow, he would never have to pay for any of the milk, and meanwhile the señora would be doing all the work, feeding the cow, taking care of it and her son, Tonio, would do all the milking. That Bobolo!

"But, Señora," Bobolo said. "I must insist that you build a wall between your property and mine to keep out your wandering animals. That is my condition: no wall, no half cow."

"You are very good, dear Signor Bonomo. I will see what Tonio and I can do. You mean well, Signor, my neighbor Bonomo." She did not see what an astute bargain her neighbor had crafted. His calm and assuring manner convinced her of his beneficent intentions. She patted him affectionately on the shoulder, her eyes brightening. Fiammella pointedly closed the oven door.

"Beatrice," said Bobolo, "run to my chamber, please, and bring us a flask of zinfandel. We will drink to the repose of the soul of Clementina."

Bobolo set his gun against the wall and then graciously seated himself at Fiammella's work table with Sandro. He motioned Fiammella and Señora Morello to sit down also. Beatrice returned with the wine and four glasses, for the Señora, Papa, Mama and Sandro. The room was quiet and expectant, for Bobolo wore his customary air of an event about to happen. He lifted his glass and, in the tones of one addressing a vast banquet hall of a Roman Emperor in days gone by, he proposed his toast.

"To all cows, from the impassioned Io and Europa of Greek Mythology to our late virtuous, dearly departed Clementina! May her udders that yielded precious white milk, more nutritious even than the celestial purple juice of divine grapes, rest in peace. *Viva il latte* (Hooray for milk) and may we always savor the milk of human kindness." He crossed himself, bowed his head and said "Amen."

Chapter 7

THE OPERA SINGER

Bobolo often needed a larger area for the exercise of his jocose soul than the arena of the Alviso hilltop. At least once a month, usually following Vesuvian eruptions when Fiammella would hint more emphatically than ever that his presence was annoying and dispensable, he fled to the city of San Francisco. "To drum up trade, my dear, to expand our business," was his ostensible excuse. But his friends knew that he sought respite from his scolding spitfire, strongly needing to regenerate his soul while living to the beat of his own drum of mirth.

On a certain morning in April 1910, he fled to the city. Three nights later, shortly after the arrival of the midnight train from San Francisco, he slid back into bed beside his Little Flame, who did not choose to recognize her mate's materialization. Yet Fiammella always missed him more than she cared to admit even to herself, and was usually as soft and sweet as *cotognata* (quince jelly) for a short while after his return.

In the early dawn, Bobolo had a moving tale to tell. His consort listened at first without any critical outbursts, so touching and persuasive was his story.

"Fiammella, my dear, I have brought back a most interesting and tragic guest. One who has fallen on sad, sad days, one to whom it is our bounden duty to be very, very kind." So far so good. "I want you, especially, to be kind to her."

"To *her*? A woman is it? How dare you? How dare you walk in here at midnight with a strange woman? How late did you stay up with her before coming into *my* bed? You *diavolo dei diavoli* (devil of devils)!" she choked, strangled by her own anger.

"Calm yourself, my beloved. She is a middle-aged, broken down opera singer, a close friend of our San Francisco friend, Mimi Imperato, who begged me to look after her. She was once a very famous opera singer of Naples, Signora Tosca Parrota. I met her at Mimi Imperato's singing restaurant the night before last, when Passerino and I had dinner there together. Her health has been very bad recently and her voice, once so glorious, is cracking up."

"I never heard of her."

"You never heard of Tosca Parrota? Where have you been, my dear? Don't you remember when the Duke of Battilocchi died by suicide, leaping from the railing of the first box to the stage of Naples Opera House when she was singing?" Bobolo barely paused before continuing. "You don't? Well, no matter. The other night at Mimi's they asked her for a song and the poor prima donna tried to sing the mad song from *Lucia*. But the diva's voice cracked like a boat in a storm. It was a good try, a mad try, a forlorn try. We all applauded because she's such a lovable soul but she left the platform in abject humiliation. Many who used to know her in years gone by were overcome with tears. You could see that she must have been a very great singer in the past. It was very moving."

In spite of herself, tears were threatening to form in Fiammella's eyes. She wiped at her face with the sleeve of her nightgown.

"Well," continued Bobolo. "Mimi and Passerino and I cooked up a little scheme for her to come down here and rest for a week or two. If we can restore her health and her voice, Mimi will give her a regular job singing at her popular restaurant. That was why Passerino and I brought her here on the train with us last night. I know you will agree that this was a good plan."

"Well, it's rather sudden but I agree we should be kind to the poor soul. Will she pay her board?"

"Not for the first three days. After that, yes."

"I see you've committed yourself, as usual. But perhaps it's a good charity."

"Yes, a very good charity. The best possible. She'll feel better and so will we. I know you'll be kind to her, Fiammella. You have a very kind heart. You will, won't you?"

"I hope I'm kind. Yes. If she's an artist in poor health, this is just the place for her."

Bobolo gave his wife a grateful hug.

In the morning they got out of bed and dressed for the day. "I'd like to have you take breakfast to Madame Parrota yourself, as a special courtesy from the Bonomo Country Inn's hostess, instead of sending the girls up to her room. Of course, she'll have to stay in her room and rest for several days."

"*Va bene* (All right). *Va bene.*"

An hour later, when the guests of Bonomo Country Inn had been served their breakfast, Bobolo came to his wife in the kitchen and informed her that the famous diva was now awake and ready for her breakfast.

Fiammella, who did have a very kind heart beneath all her vehemences, prepared a deluxe tray of freshly made Italian bread, unsalted butter, honey, prosciutto, scrambled eggs and coffee. Beatrice added to the damask-covered tray a lovely yellow chrysanthemum from the garden. Beatrice and Laura, eager for a glimpse of the famous prima donna, followed their mother and the tray. Prompted by Bobolo and aware of an "occasion," Passerino, Sandro and half a dozen of the inn guests had ranged themselves on the benches around the rear yard. The front window of the guest chamber above Bobolo's Chamber of Mirth stood open.

As Fiammella and the children came into the open space in front of the guest house, the sound of mutilated, high-pitched singing came through the window. The poor prima donna was trying to sing. Her voice was pitifully fractured, painfully determined, heart-breaking. At first the voice was stuttering but gradually syllables and then words became audible. "Mario! Mario! *Mio amor!*"

These were words from Puccini's opera *Tosca*. Fiammella stood still. One could not enter the poor prima donna's room before the sad song was finished. *"Io, son - io. Che cosi tor-tur-a-to!"* she sang as if she were indeed expiring with grief. A swan-song. A death-song surely. The straining notes tore at Fiammella's heart. Tears began to form in her eyes and splash upon the flower that Beatrice had placed on the tray.

"Mario! Mario! *Su presto. Andia-mo, andia-mo* (I am going). *Su mor-to, mor-to* (I am dead, dead)!" shrieked the sad voice in heart-felt agony.

Bobolo looked out of the upper window. He saw Fiammella hand the tray to Beatrice and pull her apron up to her eyes to catch the tears. He saw Beatrice pass the tray to Laura that she, too, might weep uninhibitedly, until Laura, too, succumbed and handed the tray to Tranquillino. The guests watched the drama with interest and sympathy, all except Passerino who stood from his bench and paced the yard.

"Oh, Mar-io! *Mor-to*"! repeated the strangled voice once more. Then the aria ceased abruptly.

Bobolo softly whispered, "Ps-s-st," put his finger to his lips and, leaning out of the window, motioned to Fiammella to come in now quickly. The tray passed back down the line, like a bucket brigade, up to Fiammella. Giving her eyes a last pat with her apron, she took the tray and began to climb the outside flight of steps that led up to the guest chamber.

As Fiammella arrived at the top of the stairs, Bobolo flung open the door with a dramatic gesture. Fiammella entered with her laden tray. The three children crept up the stairway and watched through the screen.

Fiammella expected to see the prima donna lying in or on the bed, exhausted from her pitiable effort at the song. But the bed, smooth and covered, was unoccupied. Fiammella looked to every corner of the room. There was no one to be seen except Bobolo who was standing at the window with his elbows extended as if he were holding something in his hands. Peals of laughter came up from the yard.

"*La prima donna!* Where is she?" cried Fiammella.

"Here!" said Bobolo. He was holding a gilded cage. "Is she not wonderful? I present to you La Signora Tosca Parrota!" In it was a beautiful emerald green parrot with a saucy pink beak, an impudently tilted head and the eyes of a crafty old hellion.

"By all the sinners in Purgatory and all the saints in heaven, is *that* who was singing, you fiend incarnate?!"

"Yes, my darling. Did you ever hear a bird sing operatic arias before? She is the most accomplished parrot in the world! The leading *papagallo* (parrot) of San Francisco! She has listened to the opera stars at Mimi Imperato's singing restaurant all her life and she can sing not just one but many arias. Are you such an accomplished singer, my love? I have heard you hum the tones of several famous operas … but can you sing them? Can you, my precious? If not, she could be a perfect companion for you! I bought her from Mimi last night. Every word I told you is true. She's an aging opera singer with a cracked voice and failing health. She needs to live in the country — with us! Ah, *mia cara Tosca* (my precious Tosca)! I love you — *con passione!*"

"*Con passione! Con passione!*" repeated the bird.

There was the sound of surprised laughter from below. The appreciation started the bird again. "Mario! Mario! *Mio amor!*"

"No, no," corrected Bobolo, holding the cage high in the open window so that the bird was level with his face. "No, *carissima*, say, 'Bobolo, *mio amor!* Bobolo, *mio amor!*"

"Bo-bo-lo … Bo-bo-lo, *mi-o am-or!*" repeated the parrot.

There was the shattering sound of the tray and all its contents crashing in the center of the upper room. The parrot fluttered in her cage. "*Mor-to, mor-to, morto!*" shrieked the bird in an attempted high C.

"Sh-sh-sh, *cara mia*," soothed Bobolo, "*cara* Tosca, *amore mio.*"

"Bobolo, Bobolo, *mio amor!*" shrieked the parrot affectionately to her new love.

Chapter 8

DIANA THE NEW GODDESS

Leo the red Irish Setter was good enough as a companion in hunting the rapid rabbit and swift-flying lark. But as Bobolo ranged farther afield every year in pursuit of bigger game — deer in the Sierras and wild boar in the Trinity mountains, he felt that he, an able and distinguished hunter, deserved a more skilled hunting dog. He decided, after discovering the kennels of a hound breeder in the hills four miles south of San Jose, that what he needed was a genuine bloodhound, a true tracker of wounded animals. He didn't want to leave wounded prey unfound. After two tours of the kennels, he selected a magnificent female hound, made a down payment and promised to return with full payment in a week.

Early the following Saturday afternoon, Bobolo filled his farm wagon with his accordion and his friends, Serafino Pipitone with his cornet, Angelo Bellucci with his guitar, and Tito Ruggero with his harmonica. Off they went, playing and singing as they traveled the dusty country roads. They put up at Merlo's house, made the welkin ring with their merriment, feasted on Matilda's great bowls of ravioli, her roast veal marinated for three deep-soaking days in red wine, her cheeses as rotund as herself, and her famous *zabaglione*, a dessert as delicate as petals of yellow roses. Her recipe was made with heated and whipped egg yolks, marsala wine and sugar, left to set and then served cold.

In the dew of Sunday morning, the five men piled into the horse-drawn wagon, drove to the kennels and called for the bloodhound. Bobolo had insisted upon renaming her Diana, Roman Goddess of the Hunt. She quickly responded to him, and he was very happy with his new friend.

All day Sunday the five men hunted in the foothills with Diana. She loved the entire process of hunting — it was in her nature. They brought back six rabbits and fifteen quail to Merlo's. The hunters cut out the breasts and handed them to Matilda for her great pastry pie. She sang as she worked, always friendly and jovial. She set down the special dish in front of Bobolo, who cut and served the aromatic pie to his friends.

"What a wonderful feast!" cried Chef Tito on his day off from cooking.

"What an amazing wife!" said Serafino, newly recovered from being a ghost. His own wife was loyal and devoted but was quite shy, rarely laughed or participated much in a social gathering.

"Yes, a truly remarkable wife," cried Bobolo, whose own wife could match the cooking but not the light, untroubled disposition.

Early on Monday morning, while the moon still hung in the sky, the friends said goodbye to Merlo and Matilda and piled into the wagon again with Diana. Still singing and playing like a band of troubadours, they returned across the pacific countryside to Alviso. Diana now and then made restless movements as if, in her enthusiasm, she would leap out of the cart. But somehow they found room for themselves, their new hunting dog, their instruments and all the space in the world for song and laughter — a veritable wagon of mirth.

By the time they reached Alviso, Bobolo felt that he was truly the happiest man in the world. He had the finest, merriest friends, a thriving family, the most comfortable home with the most savory kitchens, the happiest room of refuge and fairest Tuscan view this side of Italy. And now, with Leo and Diana, Airone the horse and Tosca the parrot, he had the most faithful of animal companions who embraced his every thought and wish … and never talked back. He already loved Diana. He could hardly wait to make his triumphal entry into the inn-yard and introduce her to his family and guests. Fiammella had no forewarning about the addition of Diana to the menagerie. He would rather not alarm her unduly beforehand about any potential new addition to their coterie. Better to ask forgiveness than permission, Bobolo knew.

They left Tito off at the Chichester house. Angelo and Serafino agreed to accompany Bobolo home.

"Play! Play!" cried Bobolo. "And sing! We will make a triumphal Roman entry into the yard!"

As the cornet and guitar expressed themselves, the trio sang the most joyous of Italian airs. It was almost breakfast time and everyone at the inn was already up and dressed. Guests and family alike moved outside to see what the jolly hullabaloo was about. The children and Leo the Setter also rushed to the scene. Fiammella, hot from her work over the stove preparing breakfast, emerged from the kitchen, sausage-fork in hand, a customary look of disapprobation in her eyes.

The first faint, tickling doubt began to quiver the ends of Bobolo's broad red mustache. But then, from Bobolo's chamber, Tosca cried out excitedly from her perch with ardor, *"Eccolo, eccolo* (Here he is)! Bobolo, Bobolo! *Mio amor!"* The welcome gave him back his courage.

In a commanding voice, Bobolo called out to his newest charge. "Come, Diana. Come to Papa!" Diana jumped from the wagon and bounded to him. "Look, Mama. My new bloodhound, Diana. Isn't she magnificent?"

"Bloodhound? Bloodhound? *Che orrore!* What a horror!" cried Fiammella.

Diana must have smelled the sausage meat on Mama's fork. With a great bound she leaped towards Fiammella, smacking two fore-paws against Mama's two breasts. Mama lost her balance and bounced to her hind side with an embarrassing, *"Oooof!"*

Bobolo rushed to the rescue. Diana was already leaning in, licking Mama's cheeks fondly. Mama was flailing with the fork and uttering maledictions. "Foul hound! Hound of the devil! Off of me. Bobolo, Bobolo! Take her off! She'll eat me alive. The devil take you, you foul beast! Bobolo, you demented bringer of more and more pets!"

Bobolo nudged Diana aside and assisted his lady up. He squeezed her arm with emphasis as he helped her to stand erect. In a quiet voice, he urged his wife, "Stop making a scene, Fiammella! The dog stays. She is my hunting dog. It's time to call the guests to breakfast."

The calm determination of her husband's voice quieted Fiammella. With a flushed face she returned to the kitchen, gave a final poke at the sausages and rang the hand-bell vigorously for breakfast. Holy saints! How much she had to endure! Now it was another dog, a bloodhound that would eat as much as three people combined! How could any one man think of so many different ways to make life difficult and wretched? And yet, as always, below the irritation, a little part of her was amused and a tiny part secretly admired Bobolo's perpetual, unquenchable joy, something she knew she was lacking.

Bobolo's affection for Diana increased. She was a beautiful hound, glossy red and tan, mellow eyes, humanly intelligent, loyally devoted. Diana, Leo, Airone and Tosca. He admired them each, spent much time with them, petted them, fed them like royalty, talked to them as if they were human and trained them to do tricks. The kids also loved the coterie with unbridled affection.

Diana had already proved her worth on brief rabbit and bird hunts. She was almost ready for the big adventure of a deer hunt. One Sunday afternoon, after a number of days when Diana had followed him up and down several hills of the Coast Range and had gathered a good many cockle burrs and considerable dust and dirt on the way, Bobolo decided to give her a bath. He set up a wooden tub in the rear yard, brought out pans of water from the house, which Fiammella, not without protestations, had to heat on the stove, and the best of bath towels, soap and sponges. The rite was duly performed. Then Bobolo sent Beatrice to the master bedroom to fetch a bottle of Fiammella's cologne.

When Fiammella walked out to see how the bath was going, she surprised Bobolo in the act of pouring quantities of her best cologne on a sponge and patting Diana all over with it. This was too, too much! It aroused not just anger but a peculiar kind of jealousy deep within Fiammella, a hidden wish to be pampered and adored like the hound in the tub, to *be* the hound in the tub, recipient of caresses and endearing terms that her husband so effusively lavished on a mere animal. She put her hands on her hips and protested. "A perfumed bath for the hound! You treat her like a *donna mantenuta,* a kept woman! Disgusting."

Bobolo jerked upright in surprise but recovered quickly. "To me she is as beautiful as a woman. Look at her — the sleek thighs, her well-turned legs, her patrician head, her beautiful drooping ears, her auburn-tawny hide, her glowing, tender eyes." He nestled his head against Diana's dramatically. This was a mistake.

No one noticed at this moment that Lady Chichester, furbished in charming but outdated clothes of the nineties — a gray lace dress and silk duster cloak accented by a lavender boa, gloves, hat and parasol — had meandered from the roadway at the front of the house to the rear yard. She paused at the corner of the house, enchanted by the domestic scene — husband, wife, just-scrubbed dog which the husband was so demonstrably doting on.

"It is disgusting, I tell you!" cried Fiammella, her voice shrill. "It is hideous! It is unnatural to love a dog like that, a beast. You have lost your soul, Bobolo Bonomo. You neglect your wife and children and shower your attention on parrots and dogs. You good-for-nothing ass of a donkey!"

Bobolo had, before this moment, been feeling very happy. Diana looked like the huntress queen that she was. Soon he would be off and away with her into the mountains, into the wonderful peace of pine forests where nothing scolded except squirrels, nothing screamed except blue jays, and no damning tongue of a woman could reach him.

He stood up and, surveying Diana with satisfaction, declared, *"Anche questa è fatta, e fatta bene, come disse quel uomo che strangolò la moglie* (Even this is done, and done well, said the man as he strangled his wife). I regret, my dear Fiammella, that you do not like my dog. Love me, love my dog, you know ..."

"I don't like your dog and I don't like you!"

"It's different with me, my dear Fiammella. I have room in my heart, plenty of room, for you and all my animals." Bobolo then seized her around the waist, lifted her high in the air, and set her down. He gave her a big hug and released her.

"Poltrone! Fool!" she persisted. Her eyes were brimming with tears.

At that moment Bobolo caught sight of the onlooker. "Lady Chichester!" he exclaimed, hurrying towards her with friendly enthusiasm. Abashed, Fiammella hurriedly tried to set straight her apron, her hair and her unhappy face.

"My dear Mr. Bonomo, how good to see you. I came up to spend a night or two in my ark and to see how you have fixed up my hill. I didn't mean to intrude upon such a ... charming domestic interaction."

"It is never an intrusion when you come, dear Lady Chichester. Be assured of that. It is a privilege. It is joy! By the way, do let me present to you my dear wife, Signora Fiammella Bonomo."

Fiammella made her way forward, gave a kind of little curtsey and extended her hand. Mrs. Chichester extended her gloved hand a little slowly and reluctantly.

"How do you do. So, you are the fortunate wife of Signor Bonomo? I wonder if you have any idea how lucky you are, Signora Bonomo, to have so charming, so gallant, so witty, kind and cheerful a consort as your husband? I would give all my riches, my house with its hundred rooms and all its furnishings, my jewels, my everything, to be able to live with a man half so gracious and cheerful and kind — in a shanty or hut or in my little ark on the hill."

Bobolo bowed like a courtier and kissed her hand.

Tears of anger, penitence and humiliation threatened Fiammella's eyes. She offered a quick bow, then turned and hurried back to her kitchen. What next, oh unmerciful heaven? Why was it that she, who works unendingly, who uses every ounce of her energy and her best intentions to make a comfortable home for her husband and children, to keep an inn besides and earn most of their income, should always be so much less loved, so much less admired and less approved of by everyone — by her children, her inn guests, her friends and now, by absolute strangers — less loved than Bobolo who spends far more time idling than working, who contributes so little to their own world on the hill?

She had a flash, wing-quick, of guilt, a recognition that what he was creating here was substantial, though built with his spirit, by tools that were intangible. Fiammella looked at her own tools, her hard-working hands. Then she sat down at the kitchen table and gave herself over to a quick flood-moment of self-pitying weeping.

A large warm object thrust itself across her lap. It was the sweet head of Diana, come to comfort her ... or was she smelling meat on Fiammella's hands again? Needing affection badly, Fiammella chose to believe that the motive was indeed affection. She laid her own head across Diana's and finished her tears there.

Diana did not try to hurry the moment. The new goddess on the hill was busy forming warm bonds with her mistress, who strongly needed her also.

Chapter 9

COUNTRY INN DRAMA

Fiammella and Diana had become such peaceable friends that Bobolo soon dared to go off on another of his happy jaunts to San Francisco, this time in mid-week. He stroked the wings of Tosca, petted and patted the two dogs, especially Diana, swirled Fiammella in a merry hug, kissed his children and was off to the city.

There was no mischief in his heart, only the prospect of making some purchases for his place in the country, drumming up a little business and enjoying some incomparable evenings with friends at Coppa's, Delmonico's, Sanguinetti's and Mimi Imperato's place, especially the latter with its attractions of excellent food followed by music, songs and skits. But mischief was to develop from the outing. Devilry seemed to follow Bobolo like his shadow or, still more, like frolicsome foam dancing in the wake of a ship cutting through a phosphorescent ocean.

It was a joyous evening at Mimi's. There were not only the usual opera singers present but a group of Italian actors. An extra female was needed for one of the impromptu Italian skits, derived from the great *Commedia dell'Arte* plays introduced to the world in the 16th Century by Italy. With no actresses available, one of the young male actors was persuaded by Mimi to equip himself as a female from her large collection of costume trunks. He did so and became a very presentable actress for the evening. In the midst of his performance, Bobolo was struck with so peculiarly merry an idea that he very nearly spoiled a love scene with his sudden laughter.

At the conclusion of the dramatic sketch, Bobolo invited the young female impersonator over to his table for drinks. After a couple of gin and tonics, Bobolo offered him an invitation to be his guest for the weekend at his Italian resort in the country. Emo Bacciardi, the young actor, accepted immediately and with pleasure, for he was temporarily out of a job and a weekend of good food with an obviously merry host sounded like fun.

"But I have one condition attached to my invitation," amended Bobolo.

"Yes, Signor Bobolo, and what may that be?"

"That when you arrive, you be attired as a young woman and carry the impersonation through that first evening, giving a little program of dramatic sketches after dinner as if you were indeed a woman in real life. I have three or four old cronies who dine with me almost every Saturday evening in a special room at my inn, and I want you to flirt with them outrageously. They are harmless but what a hoax! What fun! A real *cena delle beffe*, a banquet of jests!"

"Well … let me think." Emo pondered the idea. "Yes," he decided. "I guess I could do that. It's all new to me though … such a situation could lead to embarrassing predicaments if carried too far. But if the disguise is to last for just one evening, I think I could carry it off with what talents I have. It might turn out to be interesting and enjoyable for me, too!"

"*Bravo!* And I'll pay you for all of this, of course, including costuming expenses. *Va bene?"*

"*Va bene.* Thank you, Mr. Bonomo. It's a deal." He clasped Bobolo's hand across the table and lifted his glass in a pledge: "To our escapade!"

"To our comedic caper! And to you, *Emma* Bocciardi!"

Bobolo telephoned to his friends in the country to meet at his house for dinner on Friday evening instead of Saturday, for he had a nice surprise for them. He also telephoned Fiammella to have an especially good meal prepared to serve in his happy Chamber of Mirth, for he was bringing a guest.

"Another parrot, no doubt."

"No, but another friend of Mimi."

"I wonder," said Fiammella before hanging up.

Fiammella was scarcely prepared emotionally for the arrival of Bobolo with a beautiful young creature, be-ribboned and be-plumed, leaning on his arm. Her hips swung back and forth like a bell in a firehouse. Who was she?

What she was, was plain to be seen. Why did Bobolo have to flaunt this brazen young creature before the entire community? Especially before his virtuous, decent wife and daughters? To bring a screeching parrot from Mimi Imperato's entertainment restaurant was a minor offense. But to bring a painted woman-of-the-night to excite his old cronies was an absolute outrage! Bobolo did not even stop to introduce her to Fiammella but took her straight to his refuge where Angelo, Tito, Serafino and Passerino were already waiting.

Fiammella got progressively more perturbed about the situation as she prepared supper. Her spoons and ladles beat a tattoo of rising indignation in the hot kitchen. But she could do nothing to deter either Bobolo or the woman. She sent Tranquillino in with the food.

In Bobolo's room, Emo was putting on a very realistic act. His imitation of a female lure-for-all, Emma, was superb. Bobolo's friends sat with those gleaming bulging eyes, pushed-up eyelids and brows, and pursed and parted lips that the proximity of a beautiful female often produced in the male.

Even Bobolo played up her allure and, now and then, reached across Angelo to lay his hand affectionately on Emma's hand or to put his arm around her shoulder. Angelo and Serafino seemed to be the most deeply affected. There was eager competition between them in suing for the lady's attentions and affections. Bobolo had surmised that such would be the case and had therefore seated the fair charmer between them.

"But where may we see you on the stage? Where will you be performing next?" asked Angelo.

"Ah, who knows?" replied Emma, winding a roll of spaghetti around her fork. She had a robust appetite. "I am, alas, at the moment, out of a job."

"But how could anyone so attractive, so gifted, so enchanting be out of a job?" purred Angelo.

"How indeed?" asked Pipitone with a vehemence to make up for his inability to match Angelo's rhetoric. "The managers in San Francisco must be idiots, total idiots!"

"It is not the fault of the managers, my dear Serafino. It is simply the general situation. Money is getting tight and people are not going to the theater as much as they did in the early days of San Francisco. But do not worry, my dear Angelo and Serafino. I never lack ... friends," she sighed and cast up her eyes towards Bobolo's new pink chandelier above the table.

The men released that staccato, gusty, quickly-inhaled laugh which always betrays that sex has been the subject of titillation.

"Ah, *bellissima donzella* (most beautiful young lady)," murmured Angelo, and laid a warm hand over Emma's sturdy hand.

Not to be outdone, Serafino resorted to that intimate little Latin gesture of slipping his hand delicately under the table and pinching Emma's thigh, a few inches below the hip.

Emma jumped slightly and gave a startled little contralto laugh. Serafino chuckled, too. It was all very confidential. Perhaps ... if he crept into Emma's room tonight instead of going home to his eel-cold wife ... Ah, divine joy! Angelo was entertaining the same thoughts and his face began to wear that tender-lipped, fawn-eyed, love-weakened look that bespeaks total captivation.

Bobolo was having the time of his life. His eyes twinkled. His red mustache danced. His feet tapped jauntily under his chair. His cheeks flushed with wine and merriment. Then he seemed to have a sudden idea. He leaned forward towards the actress.

"Dear Emma," he said. "Now that the time for fruit and sweets has come, I wonder if I could persuade you to go with me into the main dining room and let me introduce you to the other guests? Perhaps you would do one little recitation for them, a reading of some beautiful romantic poem, some love-scene from a play? Perhaps it will be the beginning of talent programs at the Bonomo Country Inn such as those at Mimi Imperato's place."

Emo was by now quite enjoying his role. His innards were warm with richly sauced Italian food and his brain was pleasantly purpled with wine.

"*Certamente*, certainly, my good friend. Anything you say. Friendship obliges and I shall be glad to share my art with your guests."

From the open-doored kitchen, Fiammella saw her husband cross the yard towards the main dining hall supporting the silken elbow of the outrageous woman, closely followed by his cronies. What was he up to? Bobolo and his friends usually kept to their own precincts. What effrontery was this to march casually into Bonomo Country Inn's main dining room, in attendance upon that actress, that *impertinente*, that wanton woman? Fiammella tidied her hair, put on a fresh apron and stalked into the dining room to see for herself.

Bobolo had conducted the actress to one end of the dining hall. His friends sat down at an empty table in the front corner. A hush came over the fifty patrons. The Bonomo children crept quietly into the room and sat on the floor. It was an attentive audience. Fiammella strode to an empty seat at a table near the one where Passerino, Tito, Angelo and Serafino were settled.

"My dear friends," Bobolo was saying, spreading his hands in a gesture almost of benediction. "We have the extraordinary good fortune of having with us tonight at Villa Bonomo one of the most charming of our Italian actresses, Emma Bocciardi, who comes to us straight from her latest successes at Mimi Imperato's famous restaurant in San Francisco. She has played all over the world, in France, Italy, Spain, South America, New York, and Boston. This distinguished actress has consented to do a little dramatic sketch for us. Please give the lady a hand."

There was enthusiastic applause. Bobolo seated himself at the table with his friends, without looking at Fiammella's flushed face, although her presence had not escaped him.

Emma bowed prettily, so that the pink ostrich feather in her blonde hair waved as with a sudden breeze. Her long-waisted, short-skirted dress of pink silk was belted with a velvet rose-colored ribbon. Her waist was pinched in, her hips full, her chest perhaps a trifle flat. But one couldn't have everything, could one? Her face was like a rose. She was all-enticing animation.

Emma recited several of the most impassioned scenes from Sem Benelli's libretto of Italo Montemezzi's opera, *The Love of Three Kings.* Her rich contralto voice throbbed with emotions. The men in the room leaned forward in their chairs, the look of arousal on their faces. Even Bobolo looked seduced. The heart of Fiammella began to beat angrily when she noted Bobolo's eager face.

> *Dammi le labbre ...*
> *Senza le tue labbre non ho pace ...*
>
> Give me your lips ...
> Without your lips there is no peace for me.
>
> *Mio cuore ardente! La tua bocca é un fiore*
> *d'ogni momento ... Si, perch'io lo colgo*
> *ad ogni istante e sempre fiorisce!*
>
> My heart of fire! Your mouth is a flower,
> An eternal flower ... For, while I gather it,
> It renews itself again and again
> For me to take!

The men in Emma's audience looked as if they were ready to leap into bed with her, even Bobolo, who was putting on a great act himself. When she bowed to finish, the enraptured audience called for more. *"Ancora! Ancora!"*

Bobolo rose, approached Emma and kissed her hand, lingering tantalizingly over it.

"More, divine Emma. *Ancora!"* he pleaded with a public smile.

Emma assented. She proceeded to give her enraptured audience an ardent quotation from Giacosa's *La Partita a Scacchi*, a chess game featuring historical characters. This, too, dealt with love and kisses.

> *Hai tu mai pensato che si possa morire*
> *Prima diaver provato che cosa sia l'amore?*
>
> Has it ever occurred to you that one might die
> Before ever having tasted love?

Fiammella noted well that Bobolo's expression was familiar, the look he had bestowed upon her years before in Italy when he had been infatuated during their courting days. Fury grew and swelled within her. She could have walked up to that Emma Bocciardi and pulled those wobbling pink plumes from her head and yanked out great hunks of her bleached lemon hair! She could imagine the thick strands of hair in her hands. She clenched her fists under the table and dug her fingernails into her palms.

The diners begged for still more recitations. *"Ancora, ancora! Evviva, ancora!"*

But finally Emma shook her fair blonde head and turned to Bobolo. "Bobolo, *caro*, dear Bobolo, I am tired. *Basta*. It is enough."

Bobolo rose. "That is enough, my friends. Emma has given generously of her talents and we thank her."

In a final mischievous impulse, in full sight of everyone, Bobolo threaded his arms around Emma Bocciardi and held her in an extended hug. She did not try to withdraw. They were prolonging the show of affection preliminary to Bobolo's dramatic disclosure of Emma's identity as Emo, when Fiammella leaped from her place at table and walked stridently up to Emma from behind.

Thrusting her hands quickly above Emma's hair, she yanked off the pink plumes. Then she enmeshed both hands in Emma's blonde hair and pulled hard. Off came the wig entirely, into Fiammella's frozen hands, and there stood Emo Bacciardi, clearly revealed as a man with his own sleekly combed black hair.

For a moment no one moved or said anything. Silence. Then the room rocked with laughter, as did Emo. Bobolo doubled over, his red mustache almost dusting the floor.

Straightening up at last, Bobolo chortled, "Let me present my excellent actor-friend from San Francisco, Emo Bacciardi! Has he not proven himself a consummate actor, worthy of being on the world's stage?"

In response, there was wild applause.

Seconds later, the wig was unceremoniously hurled by Fiammella into Bobolo's smiling face. The only member of the audience not amused by Emma Bacciardi stomped out of the room with a yowl of anger from her flushed, chagrined face. Fiammella's jealousy and rage had once again made her look like a fool, adding extra laughter to Bobolo's special night of entertainment for his inn guests.

Chapter 10

STINGING LESSON

In spite of the humming success of their country inn and its guest houses in the hills, Bobolo was always on the lookout for pleasant and thrifty ways of supplying the table from the surrounding natural resources rather than from grocery stores in the village below. He shot rabbits and birds and Fiammella dressed them up in flour and eggs and herbs, then broiled them on skewers with bacon until they were fit for the Dukes of Aosta or Savoia.

He gathered mushrooms (more selectively than unwise Pipitone) which were placed into the bubbling pots of sauces for spaghetti or for *pollo alla cacciatore*, that recipe for Hunter's Chicken which is not in the repertory of most American households. His own vegetable garden, now fenced on one side at Señora Morello's expense, gave a very good yield under the diligent cultivation of Sandro plus the more leisurely intermittent attentions of Bobolo. Plans were in the offing to enlarge the garden significantly.

One day, while rabbit hunting along a creek two hills away, Bobolo discovered a swarm of bees hovering around a recess of decayed wood in the crotch of an old live oak. He decided that those bees must be domesticated on his own hill, yielding their honey to his favorite Alviso entrepreneur — himself! He remembered an old Tuscan tradition that swarming bees could be lulled into captivity by the application of deafening sounds. He had a vague memory of peasants crossing fields beating on copper pans.

"Children! Sandro! We're going to bring home a swarm of bees!" he declared as soon as he reached home on the afternoon of his discovery. "Drop your work, Sandro. Never mind the tomatoes. We'll have feasts of honey such as Hybla and Hymettus have never yielded."

"Friends of yours?" asked Sandro.

"Yes, sweet old friends. Hybla, a mountain in Sicily, and Hymettus, a mountain in Greece, both known for their ancient honey production, will be out-yielded by Bobolo and Sandro! Come now, children. I want you to bring big clattery pans that will make a great noise, and big spoons and the rolling pin to bang on them. We have to march down to that creek making a noise like fifty earthquakes! When the bees are stupefied with fright by all of the hullaballoo, Sandro will simply slip a sack over them and — *ecco!* — they're ours to bring home to manufacture honey for us for the rest of our living and eating days. Sandro, get two or three of the biggest sacks you can find. Then set two big wooden boxes over there at the end of the vegetable garden. That will be our hive until we can create a better one. I think we can make the bees very happy!"

The children and Sandro moved out in different directions. Bobolo's joyous enthusiasm for a new adventure communicated its vibrations to everyone, as usual.

In ten minutes Sandro was back with the boxes and sacks. The children were back from the kitchen, already beating on their pots and pans, while Fiammella, her necessary utensils for the preparation of supper swept from the racks, was chasing after them quite uselessly. They easily outran her and had the cheerful support of their father for the hive-pilfering about to take place.

They started out on the expedition at once. Bobolo led the way like one of Garibaldi's battalion captains — head up, red mustache ruffling in the wind, a happy smile on his lips and in his eyes, his feet beating a martial rhythm to the fine drumbeat he was playing with the rolling pin on a great copper boiling pot. Leo and Diana cavorted and barked wildly alongside Bobolo.

The three children danced and skipped and ran like followers of the Pied Piper of Hamelin, to the full youthful love of din, beating on their own great metal pots and pans. Sandro brought up the rear of this caravan carrying the sacks.

Tosca the parrot, in her cage in the open window of Bobolo's chamber, fluttered her wings and sang out her newest inspiring messages. The first two of these, taught to her by her loving master, represented the very essence of his philosophy:

"Vive il vino! Viva la vita! Viva Bobolo, *mio amor!"*
Long live wine! Long live life!

The sparsely scattered neighbors looked across the fields at the loud procession. Señora Morello ran to the edge of her garden to see what the clatter was all about. Dogs barked. Blue jays and red-winged blackbirds rocketed away to safer slopes, protesting. Squirrels watched, frisked, chattered and ran away to protect their ears. And many smaller unseen creatures and insects yielded their territory temporarily to the noisy intruders.

Down through the orange poppies and golden bristles of wild oats they proceeded, past madrone bushes as red-brown as the bodies of the Digger and Ohlone Indians who had once inhabited these coast range hills, down to the creek of the first hill, up the second hill, rattling the pans and singing and shouting. As they marched towards the swarming-tree, they increased the intensity and clamor of the din, trying to match the sound of military artillery of a modern invading army.

"There they are! There they are!" shouted Beatrice as the swarming mass became visible at the heart of a live oak tree near the edge of the creek bed. The bees had not yet completely settled. A large dark seething mass of them were fairly well clustered in the lowest crotch of the tree, but winged contingents soared and veered and zoomed all around the tree.

"Eccoci! Here we are!" cried Bobolo, excitedly. "Now, Sandro! Now! Hold wide open your largest sack and, as we make our

loudest noise, you run down and quickly cover the main cluster with the sack. *Ecco!* You will take them easily!"

"But, Signor Bobolo, they haven't settled down yet. It isn't the right time to take them. They will sting me all over to protect their queen."

"*Sciocchezza!* Foolishness! The bees will be so scared of our immense noise that they will fall into a stupor. Now, children — bang your pots louder! Scare those bees into submission. *Il Capitano* Bobolo and his army demand surrender now!"

Bobolo continued to bark orders to his make-shift battalion. "Forward march, Lieutenant Sandro!"

Sandro, with terror in his eyes, inched forward on ungainly feet down the hill. He held the sack in front of him, wishing that his arms were a hundred feet long. His pervasive fright slowed him. He had hunted honey in the past, saw that the bees in front of them were roiled up and knew they should use smoke on them, not noise, for the safest capture.

"*Avanti, avanti*, Sandro! Forward, to the Great Battle of the Bees. Pretend it is the Turkish Army you are attacking! You are invincible, Sandro," shouted Bobolo. He was feeling like a General in the Greco-Turkish war. The bees were the Turks who needed to be neutralized and captured.

The children sensed danger in front of them so they tarried in the back but continued pounding bravely and loudly on their pots.

Bobolo moved forward a few feet, then came to a halt. For the first time, he became aware that their noise did not seem to subdue the bees at all. My God, he worried, is this not going to work? Should we retreat and wait for another day, another plan? No, I cannot order a retreat in our first engagement, not with this battalion. "*Avanti*, Sandro, *sempre avanti!* Forward, ever forward!"

The bees were not subdued, dropping dead or falling into coma either in the main cluster or elsewhere. They all seemed, to Sandro, alive and well and getting decidedly more defensive, annoyed and angry. He could hear their loud and forbidding buzz, which seemed to say in hundreds of voices, "S-s-s-s-stay away ... s-s-s-s-s-stay away, Sandro!"

"Now, now, Sandro!" urged Bobolo. "Throw the sack over them! Now, don't miss this chance." With a supreme effort of courage Sandro lunged forward and tried to cap the main swarm with the sack opening. But something went wrong. The bees, with an explosive *zumm, zumm, ZUMM, ZUMMM, ZUMMMM* escaped from the sides and from under the sack. They first rose in a dense black cloud, then swarmed upon Sandro, ready to give their lives to protect their queen.

They covered him, body and face. As each bee alighted wherever there was flesh, it deposited a stinger with such a jolting pain that Sandro leapt wildly, shrieked a mortal shriek and ran stumbling up the slope, not seeing where he was going. He flailed his bee-covered arms against his-bee-covered face, crying pitifully in high-pitched Italian, the language of his childhood. *"Santa Maria! Gesu Cristo! Sono morto! Sono cieco e morto* (I'm blind and dead)! *O Dio! Sono morto! Sono morto!"*

The children ran in terror in another direction. Bobolo raced parallel to poor Sandro, feeling a desperate, futile inability to help his friend. He tore off the light jacket he was wearing and used it to swat at the bees on Sandro in a frenzy himself, driving many away. As seconds slowly ticked by, mercifully, more bees began to veer off as the distance from the tree where their queen remained got greater. Sandro shouted and moaned as he continued to stagger uphill. More bees headed off and away. When Sandro finally stopped moving forward, Bobolo whacked determinedly at the remaining bees on Sandro's face, arms and legs, while Sandro tried to scrape them off with his already swollen hands. A number of angry bees flew over to sting Bobolo.

Like Saint Sebastian under a hail of arrows, Bobolo disregarded the pain of his own stings. With all his strength, he half-carried, half-pulled a stumbling Sandro, whose eyes were closed, up and down the two hills and finally into their yard. The children in a panic had already reached the inn; in a flurry of words, they had blurted out to their mother what happened. She had quickly called Dr. Nollins and told him to rush over. She got a pail of water ready and, as soon as Sandro arrived, doused his sting-hot, anguished face and arms with the cool water. The few bees still attached were whacked off by Bobolo. He and Fiammella supported Sandro into the house and laid him down on the parlor sofa. His face was a bloated red moon, his eyelids swollen shut. His neck was the neck of a giant. He was so drowsy he could no longer even moan. Bobolo quickly got a bottle of rum from his room and forced Sandro to gulp some down.

Dr. Nollins soon arrived in his new Model T Ford. He quickly examined Sandro, plied him with more rum, and asked Fiammella to bring some cold, wet towels. Carefully and methodically with his tweezers, the doctor began the difficult task of removing dozens of stingers still embedded in Sandro's flesh without pressing, if possible, any more poison out of their poison bags, part of the rear end of the bees. That all of those stinging bees would now be dead was cold comfort to the recipients of their wrath.

Dr. Nollins gravely concluded, "The poor fellow has had a severe reaction to this very serious attack, though not an allergic one. However, he has received a tremendous amount of formic acid and is gravely affected. I've known attacks like this to kill even a strong man, Bobolo. If he survives, which he may not, he may slip into coma for many hours, even a couple of days, before coming out of it. We have no specific treatment besides cold packs to reduce swelling so, if you believe in prayer, now would be the time."

"Doctor, you *must* save him," urged Bobolo. "He's a very good man, *un brav'uomo,* as we say in Italian. Sandro is *un buon tipo,* the salt of the earth."

Sandro, through the raging bee toxins flowing through him, heard the tribute of his friend and boss, which was better than strong rum for his spirit. It was the only tribute to himself that he had ever heard. "*Un brav'uomo,*" a good man. "Salt of the earth" … He, Sandro.

Under the balm of these laudatory words, Sandro began his painful recovery. Being a friend and handyman for a man like Bobolo, who thrived on pranks and adventures, Sandro knew he would risk mischance and danger at times. He had accepted this at the outset.

Bobolo put Sandro in his Chamber of Mirth to recover. As Sandro slept and mended over the days, Bobolo decided to reward him with a new title, Chief Agriculturist, at a higher salary. Ten days later, to everyone's tremendous relief, most keenly Bobolo's, Sandro went back to work.

While recovering, Sandro made up his mind it was time to double the size of the vegetable garden. And it was time to modernize. So that Bobolo would well remember the hazards to others of his wild ideas, Sandro opted to sting him for the cost of one of those new-fangled small tractors being advertised. Bobolo smiled and couldn't say no. Bobolo had been telling his other friends for years that Sandro was much smarter than people thought. Silence in conversation doesn't mean lack of wisdom … the opposite is often true.

Bobolo took a quiet moment to apologize to his friend. "Sandro, I am deeply sorry that my foolishness and ignorance about bees caused you so much misery and almost took your life. It was absolutely my fault, a very stupid mistake."

Sandro bent his head down and nodded. After a pause, he looked back up at his employer, his companion.

"Now," Bobolo continued, "we must move on. I have ordered the tractor you requested and do need." He congratulated Sandro on his excellent recovery, slapped him very gently on the back and began laughing about Sandro's impossible-to-refuse tractor request. "The Stung is now the Stinger! Well done, Sandro!"

Bobolo promised himself to learn from projects and pranks which go sour and cause more hurt than happiness. He must do more homework and preparation before moving forward with his creative ideas, as he is always advising his children to do. He must derive more wisdom and prudence from experience. It was Confucius who said that mistakes are the dues one pays for living a full life, but a man can only build a richly flavored life if he makes sure he always learns from such mistakes.

Chapter 11

THE ANNIVERSARY

On September 20th, 1917, Bobolo and Fiammella were to celebrate their twentieth wedding anniversary. Bobolo decided to make a grand occasion of it, inviting all their best friends. They would dine outdoors on long tables in the spacious yard between the house and guest houses. The many courses of food would be brought from the kitchen to a serving table under the arbor and then to dining tables arranged in a sort of wide circle in the open yard not far from the fine grape arbor nearest to Señora Morello's property.

Bobolo found it amazing that they had already been on their new property for eleven years, having moved to Alviso soon after the San Francisco earthquake of April 18, 1906. Their children were now almost grown up! Beatrice was nineteen and Laura seventeen. Little Tranquillino, more like his father every year in looks, personality and *joie de vivre*, was fifteen, tall and handsome.

Bobolo began early in July to get his place into ship-shape for the grand event. One of his hobbies, since building his house on the hill and developing Italian-style terraces where the guest houses had been set, had been making cement steps, pathways, benches and pillars. The special feature of all this cement work had been Bobolo's unique loving additions. Bespeckling every step and every stretch of walkway, every bench, he had embedded mementoes of his family and household — pieces of the children's dolls, wheels from their toy-carts, broken bits of their blue family china, small scissors, keys, rings from the harness of the faithful old horse, the tip of Clementina's horn, studded sections from the dog collars of Leo and Diana, a broken bracelet of Mama's and countless fragments of the greenish glass of wine flasks and bottles. Memories were everywhere embedded, intriguing guests as they walked around the property.

One short cement pillar at the beginning of the path to the dining hall sported an entire wine flask. Across stood its mate, a pillar enshrining a majolica plate which once held spaghetti with clams, broken by a ghost. A sign indicated that this was the "Via del Buon Appetito" ("the Way of Good Appetite"). Several paths bore the names of Bobolo's heroes of liberation: Garibaldi, Mazzini, Cavour, Massimo d'Azeglio. A bench where Bobolo particularly enjoyed sitting in the sun to think, to doze, to dream, bore the inscription *"Qui Bobolo Sana"* ("Here Bobolo is Healed").

Over the eleven years, Bobolo had steadily remodeled and enlarged the Bonomo Country Inn, crafting it entirely of local stone and brick, covering it in pink stucco similar to that of large villas in the hills above Florence, as in Fiesole. The inn now had a large three-story main structure containing the reception area, two living rooms for relaxation, and a large restaurant-dining room, capped by an inviting observation room with large windows to view the lovely "Tuscan" hills and valleys. Two longer wings at right angles, each of two stories, contained the majority of the guest rooms. In addition, the property had five smaller guest houses for families or small groups. Bobolo had imported a dozen Mediterranean cypress trees from Italy, the first in California, now growing stoutly in their typical tall, statuesque manner, adding more Italian character to the hilltop.

Now for the grand occasion of their anniversary Bobolo built a cement gateway to substitute for the old one of wood, a gateway with sturdy pillars five feet high and large imposing cement jardinières set into them. As was his wont, he hummed and sang and whistled as he worked. It was good to be alive on a hillside in California. There were nagging problems … and there were simply naggings. But, *che importa?* What did it matter? *Viva la vita — sempre* (Long live life — always)!

To Bobolo's Wedding Anniversary feast came his friends and their wives, the Ruggieris, Pipitones, Angelo Bellucci, Serafino Pipitone, Mimi Imperato, Emo Bacciardi and a host of others from San Francisco, the Petris, Fontanas, Pedrinis, Gianninis, Anita Morello and her son from next door, even the priest, Father Simeoni (at Fiammella's insistence), Dr. Nollins, some of their longer-staying guests and regular customers, the judge, the mayor and other friends from the village, the valley and both San Francisco and San Jose.

In the fullness of his heart Bobolo had even invited Lady Chichester who, surprisingly, had accepted. She sat at one end of the head table, swathed in velvet and veils, somewhat bewildered by the most informal Bohemian festivity she had ever attended. With his unfailing sense of humor and irony, Bobolo had placed rustic Sandro on one side of her and, on the other, Serafino Pipitone who feigned amorous overtures to her all evening. Oddly and to Bobolo's shocked amusement, Pipitone's flirtations seemed to arouse a reciprocal coquetry from his strange unpredictable friend Lady Chichester!

Fiammella had, of course, prepared the prodigious dinner herself — antipasto, Italian salad with lettuce, tomatoes, olives and spices, five tender young goats weighing fifty pounds each, cooked slowly after being marinated in Marsala wine for forty-eight hours. Also served were battered deep-fried artichoke hearts, zucchini stuffed with chicken with a hint of garlic marinara sauce, followed by Fiammella's famous *zabaglione* dessert, light and silky as a maiden's dream.

As the *pièce de résistance*, in addition to everything else for this feast, Fiammella had baked and meticulously decorated an enormous tiered white cake, as lovely as a wedding cake, initialed with F and B in pink butter cream and topped with a ring of delicate pink sugar roses. The children had insisted that, when everything was ready, Mama should change into her wedding gown for the party. The three Bobolo teenagers would do the serving.

Standing over stoves for large portions of her days during the last twenty years had flattened Mama's feet so much she could no longer comfortably wear her white satin wedding heels. But her wedding gown of cream satin, pressed for the occasion, still fit her well. Her daughters urged her to put on her wedding veil also, but Mama thought that would look a little ridiculous, so she wore a white Shasta daisy in her dark hair instead. After all the preparations but before the first guests had arrived, Fiammella dressed almost as carefully as a bride. She stood for some minutes before her mirror, trying to remember how she had felt when she had first worn that wedding dress.

No one, she had felt sure on her wedding day, could be more wonderful, fascinating, handsome, sturdier a protector, surer a success for the future than her selected spouse. And she would match him with the heart-felt ardor of her passion and a lifetime partnership of loyalty and teamwork. Then, the morning after the wedding and some unremembered argument during the night, the groom had followed the distant call of Greek liberty and left her to fight the Turks! Confusion, dismay and finally fury shook her again. On his return, she had magnanimously taken him back to her injured heart and bosom. Had she been a fool?

What had actually happened during that wedding night? What could she possibly have said that would trigger his precipitous departure for war the next morning? She had only misty hints of recollection. For years she had believed it had been entirely his fault but one sure nagging memory was that she *had* drunk too much champagne over the course of her wedding day and night. She maybe had a snippet of memory of screaming at him, another possibly of a shocked look on his face over something she had shouted. God forbid she had said something about her rather brisk love life in the six years before meeting Bobolo, her "promiscuous years" as she labeled them in her mind. No, she didn't want to think about any of this. It was foggy. She forced any slivers of remembrance back into her subconscious and merely remained irritated.

On the positive side, what had twenty years given her? She smiled a little wryly. They had given her a fine family, a substantial estate, very hard work, irritation, vexation almost to the extreme, but also excitement, adventure, amusement, and honestly, a rather wonderful life, busy but fulfilling. Without Bobolo she might be nothing. With him she was a thorny bush, perhaps. But with him she was *alive!* Did she love him? Most of the time, no! But down deep, yes, she must love him. God bless him ... but also the Devil take him! Do those with forked tails who conceive outlandish pranks deserve to be loved? Perhaps, especially when they love their children, which he does. And he shows great patience and even fondness for her despite her occasional short temper and prickly nature.

Fiammella touched the flower in her hair and went down to meet her groom. He was already circulating among the guests in his black wedding suit, a Shasta daisy matching hers in his lapel. Bobolo was still handsome, more handsome than hard-working Fiammella was pretty. She realized that fully. The gods were with Bobolo, always.

Bobolo came to meet his wife as she issued from the house; he bowed low, took her by the arm, told her earnestly she looked beautiful, and escorted her to the front of the head table. Several voices broke out into the tune of the Lohengrin wedding march. Bobolo squeezed Fiammella's arm affectionately.

Bouquets of daisies, stalks of greenery and a few late roses decorated each long table. Flasks of wine were abundant, one for every two places. A light above the house door and the many lanterns gave a moderate diffused light to the outdoor area. Near his own place Bobolo had placed the parrot cage with Tosca in it, for how could so great an occasion be celebrated without the presence of such a famous retired diva? Leo and Diana meandered freely among the guests without being interruptive or demanding.

The two Bonomo girls, Beatrice and Laura, wore identical aprons over pretty white dresses, looking like mature attractive young ladies ready to serve the gathering guests. Tranquillino, with his handsome Italian looks and quick wit, more and more the image of his jocund father, kept the glasses filled with wine. No one drank too much but everyone was touched with a grapey sparkle. Bobolo feigned to be a great imbiber but his natural ebullience could scarcely be enhanced by wine and no one had ever seen him drink too much. At the head of the table with the temporarily quiet but bright-eyed Fiammella beside him, he began to tell some of the old stories of the Greco-Turkish War of 1897 as the meal began.

"And there we were, my friends, in the hills of Crete, facing the fierce, the mighty, the terrible, the powerful Edhem Pasha with his 58,000 men armed with their flashing Turkish sabers and their thundering guns."

"Pass the bread down the table," suggested Fiammella.

"Yes, my love. And there we were with our small but valiant army and only nine artillery guns. It was David versus Goliath, Ulysses against the Cyclops, Alexander and Porus. We pushed ahead and, on the night of April tenth, we pressed across the frontier. Never shall I forget that night how ..."

"Pass the zucchini," inserted Fiammella.

"Ah, me. Yes, my dear ... Then we got into difficulties. The fierce Turks flashed their murderous sabers, cannonading to the right and left of us, filling the valleys with ear-splitting thunder. They managed to outflank us and started squeezing us between them. Then the magnificent Colonel Smolenski arrived to lead us. He marched us down to one of the famous passes of Crete, reminiscent of the Pass of Thermopylae, and ordered us, like Leonidas, the great Leonidas, to hold the pass ..."

There was nothing left on their end of the table to ask Bobolo to pass along. The protracted recital irked Fiammella. She considered the subject inappropriate at a wedding anniversary celebration. Among other reasons, it revived the humiliating memory of

Bobolo's abandonment at the very dawn of their wedded life, and in front of all their guests! She kicked his shin under the table but Bobolo only looked back at her with a benign and doting smile. In truth, he was playing the raconteur, regaling their guests intentionally to preclude one of her usual verbal explosions at social events. He was actually trying to protect her. So he continued with his story.

"Yes, there we were like the great immortal Leonidas at Thermopylae. The night was dark. There was only a sickle moon like a curved Turkish saber in the sky ..."

The parrot, seeking a bit of attention as a member of the head table, interjected, "Bobolo! Bobolo, *mio amor.*"

The amorous parrot pushed Fiammella past her patience; she could stand no more. *"Basta queste favole maledette* (Enough of these blasted stories)!" she attempted to stage-whisper, pinching Bobolo unmercifully on the leg. Bobolo twitched and grimaced which Angelo Bellucci up the table noticed.

Angelo smiled and decided for fun to back Fiammella and add a verbal thrust. "Yes! *Basta*, Bobolo. Enough of the Greek war!"

Serafino, who had a ghostly score to settle with Bobolo, also picked up the cue and chimed in, "Down with the Greek campaign! Down with all battles tonight, Bobolo! Down with Leonidas!"

Bobolo's good nature allowed him to take a ribbing and he accepted the hint that he was perhaps dominating the conversation inappropriately with war stories. He laughed and, lifting his glass, sang out, as if toasting the assembled throng, the first few lines of *Cavelleria Rusticana*, the one-act operetta by Pietro Mascagni:

> *Viva il vino spumeggiante*
> *Nel bicchiere scintillante,*
> *Come il riso dell'amante*
>
> Here's to the wine that foams
> Within the shining glass
> Like a lover's ecstasy.

Ai vostri amori!
Alla fortuna vostra!
Beviam! Beviam.

To your loves!
To your good fortunes!
Let us drink! Let us drink.

"Viva il vino! Viva il vino!" shrieked the parrot. Tosca's enthusiastic endorsement of the beverage gave Bobolo a sudden idea. He took Tosca from her cage, placed her on the table, and offered her his glass of wine. She had often been treated to wine at Mimi Imperato's place and loved it. Now she lapped it up in a birdy way, riffled her wings and raucously shrieked, *"Vino! Vino! Viva il vino!"* to the widespread delight of the guests. The party had certainly warmed up.

Tito Ruggiero launched into the song from Don Giovanni, *"Eh, via Buffone"* ("Come on, Buffoon")! The company at the tables joined Tito in the song which so clearly described their well-loved anniversary host.

Now, turning to Fiammella, Bobolo lifted his glass and sang Marcello's aria, *"Quella Fiamma che M'accende"* ("This Flame that Burns me"). Fiammella blushed and looked shyly pleased. Again the whole company joined in, celebrating the anniversary couple with a rousing rendition of that romantic aria.

"Fiamma! Fiammella! *Fiamma!* Fiammella!" cackled the inebriated Tosca, waddling from side to side of the table among forks and spoons. Bobolo stood to retrieve her and placed her lovingly back in her cage.

The Bonomo girls circulated to remove the plates and silverware of the main course, while Tranquillino continued to keep wine flowing until he surreptitiously retreated to his own room, temporarily. The spirited party was progressing beautifully, working towards a series of climaxes — desserts, entertainment, Bobolo's gift for Fiammella, and dancing.

When Beatrice and Laura emerged ceremoniously from the kitchen, stepping slowly and carefully, they were carrying between them Fiammella's great white cake ornamented with lovely pink sugar roses, to the appreciative *ooh's* and *ahh's* of the guests. The Palace Hotel in San Francisco could have offered nothing more magnificent.

Before the cake was cake was cut and served, a fully garbed and face-painted clown somersaulted into the grassy area in the center of all the tables. Only Bobolo and his daughters knew this was to happen.

The clown warmed up by juggling three, then five, and finally seven balls. Then from under a table he pulled out a stuffed South American spider monkey with a decidedly prehensile tail and launched into a raucous act which had everyone howling. After that, the Bonomo sisters dragged over a prodigious metal wash basin containing a greased piglet. The clown jumped in to wrestle down the piglet, ostensibly to truss it for barbecuing. A tremendous battle ensued to subdue the slippery, squealing little beast! The wild ruckus had the guests on their feet, laughing and shouting encouragement, mostly for the pig!

Alas, at last, the clown himself was "conquered" by the diminutive, though ferocious, porcine beast. The vanquished clown lay still in the basin, eyes closed as if in death, while the baby boar squealed stridently in indignant triumph. Bobolo approached the basin with Sandro; together, they hefted the unmoving clown and set him onto a wooden carrying board to prepare *him* for barbecuing. They surrounded him with potatoes handed to them by the Bonomo girls and then poured an aromatic sauce over his prostrate body. As a final touch, Bobolo wedged open the clown's mouth and stuffed in an apple.

When the laughter abated, Bobolo addressed the crowd. "What wonderful, wonderful entertainment to celebrate our special day. Thank you to our clown, our very own ..." he paused ... "Tranquillino!" And the clown leapt up from the board like a gymnast landing a vault, dripping and splattering his sauce!

Even Fiammella was surprised! Tranquillino had spent three months working at a vaguely-explained "summer job" in San Francisco, living with Mimi Imperato, secretly training full-time with a retired clown whom Bobolo and Mimi had brought in from Chicago to train Tranquillino.

The whole audience stood and cheered! Clown Tranquillino bowed lavishly, then returned to his prostrate position on the carrying board. Bobolo with Sandro's help lifted board and clown up and headed away to the barbecue. Fiammella and the guests were left to savor the exquisite cake and continue enjoying the exuberant evening.

After Bobolo and Sandro set soggy Tranquillino down, giving him slaps and hearty congratulations on his fine performance, Bobolo slipped away to his private chamber.

When he rejoined the party, Bobolo was carrying, with as much slow ceremony as that with which the girls had brought in the cake, a large hat box tied with wide white satin ribbons and topped with a splendid bow. Just as the girls had set down the cake at Papa's direction exactly between Papa's and Mama's place, Papa now set down the hat box down in front of Mama with a tremendous flourish. He stooped, gave her a big kiss on the forehead and, in a booming voice, announced, "For my beautiful bride!"

Chatter at all the tables dimmed to silence. All eyes were on the big box, most with expressions of delighted expectation, though some with dubious suspicion; those who knew Bobolo best worried that the "gift" might be a hoax devised by the Prankster-in-Chief.

Mama's face shone with pleasure. Papa often had brought home little presents from San Francisco for the children but did not often bring home presents for her. Almost never, in fact. Here at last was a gift from Papa, a big and very feminine-looking gift. Was it a hat? Or fur-piece? Or a beautiful dress? What could it be? She felt very girlish and expectant, almost giddy. It was a crowning moment for her, for all to see.

"Open it, Little Flame! Open it, Fiammella!" urged Bobolo.

Fiammella stood up and self-consciously but proudly began to untie the bow. It was tightly knotted but with excited fingers she was able to open it and pull the silky wide ribbon strips off the circular box top. She waited for a second with an expression of rapt anticipation, looked out at the large group of friends and well-wishers, turned back to the box and pulled off the lid with a hopeful flourish.

She looked inside ... where there was another smaller beribboned box. Doubts began to rise inside her. She quickly reached in, untied and opened the second box without allowing herself the chance to think or worry.

Inside the second box, there was yet another smaller box.

There were a few nervous titters from the audience. But many guests began to worry in earnest, as did Fiammella, who smiled nervously. She hesitated, unsure if she should proceed. How embarrassing it would be if the final small box was empty — signifying twenty years of an empty marriage. In front of this crowd! Fiammella's face slipped from happy expectancy to tense embarrassment. She faltered, wondering if she could find a way to stop this show, but finally started opening the final very small box ... and there, nestled in a cotton puff, was a beautiful sparkling ring with a very large central diamond encircled by gleaming rubies! She actually screamed in happiness and relief and, with a huge smile, held the ring up for everyone to see. There were loud gasps of awe and admiration from the crowd. Bobolo beamed.

Fiammella took off the wedding band and small diamond engagement ring which she had worn for twenty years and one month, put the new ring on her left fourth finger, and replaced the wedding band. In that moment of utter happiness, she bent over to kiss Bobolo's welcoming lips. Bobolo rose and embraced Fiammella to the hoots and *bravos* of their gathered friends.

Here at last was a lovely, expensive token of his affection for her. Yes, he did love her, though he put her through a nerve-wracking public performance to reveal it, nearly paralyzing her!

Bobolo turned to the audience, gave a signal to his musical friends and announced that he and Fiammella would now start dancing while everyone else could either enjoy more dessert — there was still *zabaglione* and more cake — or join them in dancing. Bobolo extended his hand to Fiammella and led her out to a small dance floor in the lanterned yard. Angelo Bellucci, Tito and Serafino started playing the dance tune from *Romeo and Giulietta* and sang:

> *Su, baldi garzon,*
> *Su, vaghe donzelle,*
> *A fervida danza.*

> Up, gallant youths
> And charming maidens,
> In the lively dance.

Bobolo put his arms about Fiammella, held her closely and began to waltz. Fiammella's eyes began to water and overflow. In a singular moment of letting her guard down, she murmured into his shoulder, "Bobolo, oh Bobolo ..."

"You look truly radiant, Fiammella. The ring is just a token of my gratitude for all of your hard work and great patience during the past twenty years. I do love you and, in spite of all my pranks and jokes, I know you will always continue to love me just as Giulietta loved Romeo."

Her foot missed a step and she stumbled just a bit. As he steadied her, Fiammella found herself asking, *I will always love you ... like Giulietta loved Romeo?* He's like Romeo? Romeo, who would give up everything for his true love?

Hardly. Ruminating on that, the spell cast by the ring was broken, and her happiness was immediately interrupted.

On the dance floor, while she was waltzing with Bobolo, a seed of anger found a fertile spot in the soil of her heart and began to enlarge.

Chapter 12

SABBATICAL

Everyone agreed that the anniversary party had been a roaring success and that Bobolo, as usual, was the star of evening and originator of most of the laughter. Many danced past midnight in the congenial atmosphere. After her waltz with Bobolo, Fiammella danced with a variety of men until the last guest left at one AM.

In the aftermath of the party, however, she pondered why Bobolo only now gave her a gift of such value, after so many long years of her diligent work, seven days a week, fifty-two weeks a year, with never even a single suggestion of her deserving or needing a vacation during their fourteen years of living in Alviso as innkeepers.

"You're a lucky woman," many guests had told her during the anniversary celebration, "to have such a wonderful, happy husband." But how wonderful is it to so often be the butt of jokes and pranks, almost all of which end up being embarrassing for her, causing anger, tears and self-recrimination? His pranks did not represent innocent fun for her, only lingering discomfiture and inner torment, often for responding so self-destructively.

Even the expensive diamond-and-ruby ring he gave her — why not just give it as a beautiful anniversary present? Why must he hide it in a small box surrounded by two other boxes, so that she and a number of the guests became progressively more worried that the final box would be empty and she would once again be put into an impossible and embarrassing position of being pranked into humiliation in front of so many of their friends?

Instead of basking in the sunshine of an unusual, atmospheric and happy anniversary party, Fiammella began to ruminate over the negative aspects of their marriage. How fulfilling is endless work? How joyous can one be when one can be pranked in public at any unsuspecting moment? How lucky is a wife whose husband's definition of joy is not to spend alone-time with her but endless hours every weekend joking and laughing with male friends who call themselves "angels" but clearly aren't?

She also couldn't help wondering what she might have said years ago on their wedding night while befuddled by champagne, which drove her new husband to risk his life on the battlefields of Crete rather than spend honeymoon time with her? Did she shatter his male ego by, God forbid, unleashing details of her promiscuous years, which she had kept secret so carefully during their courtship either by silence or repeatedly lying? What business was that of his, anyway? He did only ask me about it once. Why did I so compulsively insist to him so many times that I was a virgin? So stupid of me. *Stupidissima!*

Was I the fool of all fools to allow him back into my life? There was plenty of time while he was fighting in Greece to get our marriage annulled. The Catholic Church would have immediately agreed on the basis of flagrant desertion. Why hadn't she done so and immediately fled Florence to other parts of Italy — Rome or Milan or Padua, for instance, to start a new unfettered life, perhaps even taking a university degree in architecture which had been one of her dreams since childhood?

* * *

One week later, Bobolo opened the door of his Chamber of Mirth to the fine sunlight of a September morning. He said a cheery "good morning" to his favorite parrot. Tosca lumped her feathers with joy when she saw Bobolo and let out a cheerful squawk of recognition. "Bobolo! Bobolo, *mio amor! Viva la vita!*" the parrot sang in B flat minor … on her own parrot scale.

For some reason unknown to Bobolo, after the party Fiammella had reverted to a foul mood every day, not just with Bobolo but with everyone. She continued her hard work in the kitchen, maintaining the high standards of the Bonomo Country Inn but her attacks on Bobolo became relentless and unremitting. It was as if she were saying, "Yes, you gave me a beautiful ring but why did you wait twenty years to give it to me and why did you embarrass me by surrounding the ring with three boxes and making me unwrap it embarrassingly in front of all of our guests?"

Bobolo's humor, as almost always, had the opposite effect on her. It did not elicit laughter but anger and bitterness. She had recently banished Bobolo again from her bed for some trifling offense. However, he slept quite willingly on his cot of exile in the laughing room to which he had often been relegated.

Why are women like Fiammella so lacking in that essential ingredient of life, a sense of humor, wondered Bobolo. *Che peccato!* What a shame! Why did God make Eve from a rib of Adam rather than from his funny bone? What a fine amiable world we would live in if only Fiammella could recognize the humor in it! Why go through one's brief life so somberly and unhappily?

Bobolo crossed the yard to the house and mounted the steps to the kitchen where dishes were already clacking against one another. A nice sound. If there were an after-life, that was one of the sounds he would like to hear in Heaven. There should also be, in those purlieus, the savors of coffee and frying sausages such as came through the open door of his house at this moment. He recalled Tranquillino's wonderful clown performance, rubbed his hands with a rich feeling of happy remembrance of pranks enjoyed in the past and of innumerable practical jokes and pleasures to come! But now he must try yet again to be patient with his Little Flame.

As he opened the screen door and let it slam confidently behind him, he greeted his wife resoundingly. "Ah, *dolcissima sposa* (most sweet spouse), good morning!"

Fiammella was alone in the kitchen. She went on about her work as if he did not exist. How odd — was he a ghost? Perhaps I will soon feel the same as Serafino did when we all treated him this way! Are we having spaghetti alle vongole tonight?

"Good morning, my good wife! Good morning!"

Fiammella shot him a furious look. She had evidently not mellowed during the night, making a full week of her bad mood, which was now affecting everyone in the family. Bobolo approached the stove where the sausages were sizzling.

"My sausages ready?"

"No sausages for you, Donkey Man. No food at all. Nothing. *Porcone* (Great pig)! Sausages are *from* pigs, not *for* pigs! Out of my way! Out of my kitchen! Be gone with you! For good! For good, I say! Did you hear me? You bring nothing except torment and trouble. *Addio! Addio!*" She waved the sausage fork at him in a sign of total dismissal.

"You mean you would like me to be gone out of your presence now? Or forever? To divorce me?"

"As a Catholic I can't divorce you, but if I could, I would, believe me! I am tired to the death of your jokes! To me you are not a funny man, not funny at all!"

"Then to make it easier for you, I can divorce you since I'm not a good Catholic. If that's what you want, very well."

"You can't divorce me any more than I can divorce you. But you can go away. That would make me happy!"

"All right, if that's what you want. I'll make out separation papers to make you joyful. Lord knows, I have tried to make you happy but it is not easy. Perhaps we should make it a legal separation — you may be happier that way." He retreated with great dignity from the kitchen.

Fiammella experienced a moment of panic. After all, you don't easily throw away the foundation stone of your life, even if it's wobbly and insecure. She turned back to the stove and furiously flipped sausages over and over until they were almost as hard as bones, or at least as hard as she was gritting her teeth.

Bobolo went to his room and procured a pen, ink and a large piece of white paper. All right, he'd go, for a time, perhaps for good. He was tired to death, too, of all this wrangling over nothing at all. Off to the mountains, off to the forest where he could be free of women's tongues and spears. He'd been planning to go deer hunting anyway with Leo and Diana. *Evviva!*

He sat down at his desk, took his time and wrote the Separation Agreement. It was to be an important document and should therefore be impressive in its wording. He dredged up from his memory all the legalistic language that he could remember:

> Document Pertaining to the Permanent Separation of Bobolo and Fiammella Bonomo. Alviso, California. This twenty-eighth day of September, 1917.

> Be it known to all present that whereas Bobolo Bonomo and Fiammella Bonomo were united in so-called Holy Matrimony on the twentieth day of September, 1897, in the Church of Santissima Annunziata in the fair city of Florence, Italy, and have lived together in wedlock, bedlock and altercation for twenty years; and whereas the *zizzania* (discord) has gradually increased until there is no peace, no happiness, no little moment left to fill with laughter in the House of Bonomo on Hilarity Hill, Alviso, California, these two unfortunate souls, Bobolo and Fiammella Bonomo have agreed to disagree, to sever the flesh and the hearts that were one flesh and one heart, to go their divided ways forever. So be it. Amen.

> Signed: _____
> Signed: _____
> Date: _____

On a second piece of paper Bobolo wrote his Will.

> I, Bobolo Bonomo, Esquire, being of sound mind and body on this twenty-eighth day of September, 1917, do hereby bequeath all my property, hilltop farm and vineyard, Bonomo Country Inn, guest houses, furnishings, personal belongings, horse, pet bird Tosca, etc. to my wife Fiammella. I know that she will rear our children well, for she is a good and conscientious mother. For myself I take only my faithful rifle and my unfailing and ever-amiable friends, my dogs Leo and Diana.
>
> Signed _____
> Signed _____
> Date _____

Just as he finished the document, Beatrice came in with a mug of coffee and a plate of sausages and risotto. "Oh, Papa! Mama told me you are going away. Where are you going and for how long?"

"For a time, for a time. On a hunting trip."

"Just now? When there's so much to be done around the place?"

"There's always so much to be done around our place. A man can stand just so much, Beatrice, and no more. You're a very sweet young girl to bring me breakfast. Yes, you're a good girl, Beatrice … actually a good young woman. How did you slip it out of the kitchen without Mama knowing about it?"

"Slip it out? I didn't slip it out. Mama told me to bring it to you but not tell you that it was her idea."

"Strange woman. Women are part angel and part devil. But so are men, so are men. His Satanic Majesty is a very good friend of mine."

"You mustn't talk like that, Papa, as if you were a close friend of the Devil. You are a very dear, good man, though you do torment Mama. Do you want to know what she was saying when I left the kitchen?"

"Yes, what?"

"Why does God always punish me? Why doesn't God ever punish him?"

"Little does Mama know how much God punishes me. There never was a sadder-hearted man, I venture to say, than Bobolo Bonomo at this moment. His heart is made of midnight."

"Oh, Papa, I never heard you talk this way before. I thought you were always, always happy and that your heart was made of sunshine."

"Didn't you ever hear of Canio, the grief-stricken clown in Leoncavallo's opera, *Pagliacci*? Or of the court buffoon, Gonella, who died of fright when the Duke of Ferrara pretended to behead him, when all he really did was pour a pail of cold water over the poor fool's bared neck? Or of Margutte who died of *laughter* — yes, of laughter — and gave us that ironic phrase, 'dying of laughter'? The mask of comedy, my daughter, is only the other side of the mask of tragedy. Mark the heart of a comedic person — it is half-filled with the tears of life, *lachrimae vitae*, as the old Romans knew so well how to call them."

"Oh, my dear Papa!" exclaimed Beatrice, setting the breakfast plate down in front of her father and placing a hand around his shoulder. "You are good and you are bad; you are happy and you are sad."

"Well, these sausages are good," commented Bobolo, "though Mama has cooked them a bit fiercely. She must have been pretending she was rolling me on the grills of Hell … or maybe she just wanted me to break my teeth eating them."

Beatrice leaned over and kissed her father impetuously on the thinning spot on top of his red head. For some reason tears sprang to his eyes. He brushed the tears off with the back of his hand as if he were slicking his hair.

"While I'm gone, my child, will you please look after my darling Tosca? Feed her well. Talk to her. Take her out of the cage every day and stroke her lovingly. All creatures, you know, need love and cherishing — even my poor old parrot."

"I love and cherish you, Papa, very much."

"But you often disapprove of things I do and so does Laura and even Tranquillino. Mama doesn't love me at all, or at least she pretends not to. So you see, even in the midst of a good sized family, I'm a lonely and unloved man. But never mind. Off in the woods I'm not lonely at all. I feel fulfilled there — with beauty, sunshine, health and joy — and the gifts of life."

"Poor dear Papa!"

"Yes, poor dear me, I suppose. Poor dear everyone on the whole wild, weeping, laughing planet when you come right down to it. Please clear the kitchen of Sandro and the children when you go back, Beatrice. I'm taking very private papers to Mama to sign. It's a matter just between Mama and me."

"Business?"

"Yes, business. And please look after Airone, too, while I'm gone. And see that Clementina the Second doesn't get into the cabbages."

"Of course, Papa."

Beatrice left and Bobolo tried to finish his breakfast. He struggled a little to swallow the risotto, not because there was something the matter with the risotto but because there was something the matter with his throat.

When he had finished breakfast and fed a few crackers to Tosca, he carefully combed his hair and mustache. He vaguely wondered why he did it. Of what possible use could grooming be now? Then he picked up the documents, read them over slowly and carefully, nodded slightly and sighed. He committed his signature to the first open line after each document and let the second for Fiammella. Since by now the kitchen should be cleared, he made his way with poise again across the yard, holding the papers and a fountain pen. Since some of the inn guests were sitting on benches around the yard or standing and chatting in guest house doorways, he hoped that Mama wouldn't yell or tear his hair or bang dishes or make any of the melodramatic scenes which had become commonplaces of life in their home. Oh, for a wife like Matilda, Merlo's placid, benign spouse! No scenes there except love-bird scenes, laughing scenes! But what did Matilda have to offer except good cooking and amiability? She wasn't smart like his Little Flame. She wasn't stimulating or spicy. She was like a round platter of spaghetti without the sauce … but she never embarrassed Merlo, only complimented him and tried her best to make him happy.

Mama was very busy washing dishes in the empty kitchen when Papa entered. Bobolo walked quietly to the kitchen table and said, "Here are the Separation paper and my Will. Please sign them as I have."

Mama dried her hands and came over to the table without even looking at Papa. She immediately took the pen and started to sign.

"Aren't you going to read them?" he asked. "You should always read a paper before signing it."

"I've read the title. It's a Document of Separation and it's a Will. That's all I need to know."

A little leaden bell tolled deep inside Bobolo's heart. In a blurred sort of way he watched Mama sign. When she put the pen down, she walked out of the kitchen into the dining room without a word. She had read neither the Separation paper nor the Will. He picked up the ink stand, pen and papers, returned to his room and put them away in a drawer of his desk. Then he began to clean and oil his hunting rifle and to pack everything he might need for a long time away from home, perhaps forever.

In addition to the barest necessities of clothing, he chose an agate ring which Fiammella had given him when they were married but which he never wore because her shrewishness had never abated. He also packed a thin paper copy of Dante's *Divine Comedy*. He would have liked to take Boccaccio's *Decameron,* too, but he only had room for one book. Besides, he felt sure that off in the woods he could supply his own merry tales and cheery thoughts, spinning the golden threads like a spider from its own insides. As he packed, he began to sing Carissimi's "Song of Freedom from Love" but he felt like Pagliacci singing with a

broken heart. He increased the volume of his tones so that perhaps
Fiammella might hear:

> *Vittoria, mio cuore!*
> *Non lagrimar più,*
> *E sciolta d'amore.*

> Victory, my heart!
> Weep no longer,
> You are free of my love (and)
> Its abject slavery.

Mama in the kitchen heard. Her tears fell with little sizzles on
the stove.

When Bobolo was all ready, his pack on his back, his gun in
hand, his dogs who knew that adventure was afoot leaping beside
him, he called Beatrice and told her to bring the other children to
him. He hugged each of them and made very light of the farewell,
although his heart weighed like a great bronze bell that would
never again swing against the blue sky of happiness.

As he set off away from Fiammella, home, children, horse and
parrot, he endeavored to sing the merry hunting song, *"Andiamo
alla Caccia"* ("We're off on the hunt")! Down the hill and across
the fields, Beatrice, Laura and Tranquillino hurried along beside
him until they reached the creek. Then Bobolo stopped, flung his
arms about as if her were scaring off birds, and cried, "Whoosh!
Home now!"

"What will you bring back, Papa?" called out Tranquillino.

"A stag bigger than Santa Claus's reindeer!"

"Really, Papa?"

"Maybe. Remember, Tranquillino, that life is made of *maybe*'s!
Addio, addio!" Bobolo strode across the creek and into the distance
without looking back, singing from Giuseppe Verdi's famous
opera, *La Traviata*: *Sempre Libera!* "Forever free I wander ..."

Chapter 13

MISSING LAUGHTER

It was one of those late October days when Nature seemed to lie on the hill slopes and recapitulate all her history of beauty. The golden brown California hills of fall looked and felt like the Tuscan hills as rarely before, with the same gentle contours, the same texture of folded gold velvet, the same blue veil-of-the-Madonna haze resting with a light touch upon them. Only the accent of the horizontally spreading live oak trees differed as always from the familiar vertical thrust of Italy's tall cypress trees which now could be seen on the Bonomo Country Inn property but nowhere else.

Fiammella paused for a moment at the bake-kitchen door and looked off and away past the vegetable garden and over the slopes where Bobolo had disappeared six weeks before. It had been a month and a half of the darkest loneliness. Without Bobolo, the inn remained efficient but sapped of spirit. Even the children, even the constant stream of guests could not seem to arouse its usual jovial atmosphere. Bobolo, it was clear, made everything alive. He was the heart and soul of the place. His laughter, his jests, even his tricks, his considerable amount of work, his innovative plans for the future, his help and his counsel with the children, his frequent loving remarks to her whether sincere or not, his energizing of everything — all had engendered the vitality of the hill. When these were taken away, it was as if the sun were gone.

No wonder Tosca, the poor parrot, had paid him the ultimate tribute of pining away to death without him. No wonder the children asked every day when Papa was coming back. No wonder Sandro, overworked, threatened to leave. No wonder Papa's friends kept dropping in to ask for news of him and then retreated sadly, the inn having little to offer the human spirit without Bobolo.

Fiammella thought that if she should see Bobolo striding back over the hills, his gun under his arm, his dogs yapping joyously beside him, she would get down on her knees, thank the good Madonna and promise to treat her husband like an angel from Heaven all the days of his life from now on, forever.

Perhaps Bobolo had indeed decided never to come back. Perhaps she had driven him away for good. She had confessed what she feared to Father Simeoni. He had admonished her to gentle her tongue when her husband returned. For surely he *would* return. He could not live forever in the mountains. He was essentially a family-loving man, the Father assured her.

Fiammella turned back to the big table where she was rolling out pasta for the rigatoni to be served at dinner. The girls were mending linen, polishing silver, setting tables and working as sous chefs in the kitchen, preparing vegetables for her to cook or, in the case of Beatrice, to help with the actual cooking. There was a pleasant pre-prandial stir about the house and a slightly eased feeling for Fiammella with her young brood about her. But still, if she were honest, her heart felt like the crypts of the Church of San Miniato on the hill above Florence, shut away from the light of God for a thousand years.

Fiammella was carrying the tray of rigatoni to the oven when she heard dogs bark in the distance. Some undefinable note of joy, the accent of delight that always accompanied the creatures around Bobolo, told her that these might be the voices of Leo and Diana. Perhaps … could it be Bobolo? The enthusiasm of the barking dogs suggested to her that Bobolo might indeed be returning home! The scoundrel! The dear impossible rogue!

Fiammella set down the tray, almost upsetting it in her excitement, on the bake kitchen table. Beatrice and Laura, who were shelling peas, jumped up, scattering pods and peas all over the floor and raced for the door. Tranquillino was already half way down the hill to the creek. Even old Sandro was loping down the hill.

Fiammella turned back to her work. She must not show too much pleasure, too much affection. She must be cautious. Already, with the forecast shadow of Bobolo's returning presence, the specters of old troubles and old torments began to darken her rebounding heart.

The barks grew louder. Out in the pasture, Airone gave a neigh that sounded like a happy chortle. Now the excited voices of the three Bonomo progeny were audible. And then the door opened and Bobolo was crossing the kitchen with his arms spread out. He took Fiammella and crushed her to him. "My Fiammella *cara!* It was a good trip. I have shipped home crates of good deer-meat and wild boar meat and bear skins. My time was not wasted. No adventure, good or bad, my dear Fiammella, is ever futile."

She put her arms around him very tightly. "Bobolo! *Il mio* Bobolo!" Then she pushed him away. "Ah, *birbone*, you naughty one. *Caro birbone*. You've been gone a long time. We've missed you … and the place has missed you. Now get to work!"

Bobolo smiled and exited the kitchen, still followed by dogs, his three kids, Sandro and several of the guests who had heard the racket and were very eager to have their beloved host back in their midst. After exchanging greetings with all these welcomers, Bobolo went to his Chamber of Mirth. He expected Tosca to call out merrily. "Bobolo! Bobolo! *Mio amor! Mio amor!*" But Tosca's cage was empty.

He turned in dismay to Beatrice. "Where's my Tosca?"

"Oh, Papa, Papa! We took such good care of her, Mama and I. Such good care. But she simply faded away after you left. She called loudly for you all day long and made a real pest of herself. Then she called a little less loudly every day until all she had left was a little parrot whisper. Then she died, Papa. She died of grief for you."

"My poor Tosca! I really loved that bird and I am so sad she is gone. She was a wonderful addition to our homestead. She had a very special *esprit* for life and infused it happily in so many ways."

Bobolo wore a black mourning band around his left arm for a whole month and felt a real gap in his life.

Chapter 14

PROHIBITING PROHIBITION

By 1919 the National Prohibition Act had been passed. By 1920 the Prohibition Enforcement Agents were abroad in the land seeking the hiding places of the juices of joy. Bobolo Bonomo paid no attention. Why should he? Rome had abundant wine during the time of the Roman Empire and continuously up to the present. Outlawing wine was preposterous! What will they forbid next — mothers' milk? *Absurdio ridicularum est*! Which is not even Latin because I just made it up, thought Bobolo to himself … but I think I'll attribute it to Seneca.

The law was nonsense, inadmissible, irrelevant and irreverent, contrary to man's reason and man's appetite, an invasion of human privacy, his castle, vineyard and estate — an affront to man's liberty! It was absolutely intolerable to any man with Italian blood in his veins, blood permeated with *vino* for thousands of years.

So Bobolo and Sandro went on extending the vineyards, aided by the small but efficient tractor. Bobolo continued increasing the size and contents of the large storeroom in the back of his chamber where he fermented barrel on barrel of wine so that rich purple fumes seeped into his room of happiness and made its atmosphere more delectable than ever, day and night.

Word got around the countryside that wine could be bought with no questions asked and no trouble at all from Bobolo Bonomo, the pleasant character up on the hill. He concealed nothing. He sold the good beverage of his ancestors openly and abundantly at a fair price. Customers came in wagons and motor vehicles and went away, their purchases hidden deep in trunk lockers or covered with blankets. Wine was served as a matter of course with meals at the Bonomo Country Inn — Bobolo took away the "optional" on the menu and made wine mandatory, with Italy's flag next to the choices.

It was inevitable that word should reach the authorities that a "blind pig," that is a "still" or a speakeasy, was being operated up on the hill.

One July evening in 1920 after supper, when the sky was still effused with yellow light, Bobolo was playing bocce with some of the male inn guests on the new clay bocce court built on one of the terraces below the guest houses. Laura came out to him and reported that a solemn-looking man was up at the main house and wanted to see him.

"I told him you were down in the court playing bocce and suggested he might go down and watch till you finished your game. He became indignant, gave a flop to his shoulders like a chicken about to take off to the roost, then opened his coat, flashed a silver badge at me and said, 'I'm a Government Officer. You'd better tell your Papa to come here right away.' Oh, Papa, I'm sure he's one of those awful Prohibition Agents who will cart you right off to jail. Oughtn't you to hide?"

"Hide? It's his hide he'd better look after! I'll handle him. He'd better not try to investigate me or my premises! This is a free country and I'm an American citizen."

"But you *are* breaking the law, Papa. He has a Government permit to inspect our property. He'll find your wine barrels right away."

"We'll see." Bobolo put his quick mind to work. "Laura — take Diana and set her down in my room in front of the door to the storeroom. And sit nearby at the table."

"I can't, Papa. I'm helping Mama in the kitchen. Mama will have fits! I'll send Beatrice."

"All right, send your sister. Between the two of us we'll get the better of any *maledetto* (cursed) investigator!" Bobolo turned to his friends on the bocce court. "Sorry about the game, friends. I've got another kind of a score to settle at the house." Bobolo's fellow players stopped the game, winked at one another and moved up to the yard benches to catch any stray sparks from the fireworks of fun that so often materialized from Bobolo's encounters.

Bobolo stalked to the house, his red mustache bristling. Beatrice came out of the house and Bobolo whispered a few instructions in her ear. Then he strode up the steps into the house.

Standing by the fireplace in the parlor was a little rabbit-shouldered man with pale yellow hair, thick glasses and an air of pomposity that is so often adopted by men small of stature and character to balloon their fragile egos. As soon as Bobolo entered the room the little man lifted his shoulders, as if chinning himself on his own clavicles, and rose on his tiptoes to give himself added inches of height and power.

"Mr. - ah Bon-oh-mo?" he queried.

Few things irritated Bobolo more than this particular mispronunciation of his name. "No. You've got the wrong man. My name's Bónomo.

"Beg p-p-pardon, Mr. B-b-bon omo. I'm B-b-belcher. Thaddeus B-belcher."

"And what do you want, Mr. Belcher?"

Belcher hesitated, seeing Bobolo's strong, confidant demeanor. Here, thought Bobolo, was an easy adversary.

"I'm an inv-v-v-vestigator for the government." He rose on his toes again and elevated his shoulders while flapping open his vest and revealing his badge. "F-f-f-first I'll have to ask a f-f-few qu-qu-questions. Do you m-manufacture any wine here?"

"Manufacture? No. Hardly. We don't manufacture wine; God manufactures wine."

"Do you have a v-v-v-vineyard? Do you gr-gr-grow gr-gr-grapes?"

"Yes. We have grapes. Who could live without grape juice?"

"I see. You have no st-st-stills about the p-p-p-place?? No blind p-p-p-pig?"

"Nothing's still around here and our pigs aren't blind."

"Are you tr-tr-tr-trying to be f-f-funny, Mr. Bónomo? This is a very serious b-b-b-business, I want you to know." Belcher rose four inches on his toes, like a ballet dancer about to take a flying leap.

"I'm never funny," said Bobolo somberly. "They call me Mr. Gravitas."

"While it is st-still light, I will d-d-do a little investigating, if you d-d-don't mind."

"But I *do* mind. This is my property, my house, my business, my estate. Who authorizes you to trespass on my property?"

"N-n-now don't get tough, Mr. Bónomo. If you do, I can t-t-t-telephone the government office that authorizes me. L-l-l-let me p-p-p-pass."

Bobolo, clenching his fists at his side, let him pass. Thaddeus Belcher went through the house, peering into every closet. He went across the yard to the main guest dining room and then into the kitchen where Mama and Laura were working at the dishes. Bobolo winked at Mama.

"This is Mr. Belcher, Mama. A very distinguished representative of the government. He is on the Committee for the Prevention of Pleasure and the Prohibition of Enjoyment. He's making a survey of our premises."

Mama wiped her hands on her apron and said meekly, "Pleased to meet you, Mr. Belcher."

"P-p-pleased to m-m-meet *you*, Mrs. Bónomo. You certainly don't l-l-look like a law-br-br-eaking w-woman." He rose on tiptoes again.

Mama fussed with her hair as a reaction to the unexpected compliment. Laura held up a plate before her face and smiled behind it.

"And my daughter, Laura," said Bobolo. Laura removed the plate.

"How do you do, L-l-l-laura? A real p-p-p-pretty girl, Mr. Bónomo. You did w-w-w-well," and he smiled uneasily.

"I have another pretty daughter, too," said Bobolo, ready to employ all possible decoys.

"Won't you try some of these *cenci*, Mr. Belcher?" suggested Fiammella with surprising *savoir faire*. There was a tempting platter of these sugared pastry bows, freshly made by Mama, on the table.

"D-d-don't mind if I d-d-do," and Belcher picked up three *cenci* at once and began to devour them. They were dry, as they're supposed to be.

"How about some wine to go with that?" asked Bobolo.

"W-w-w-wine?" exclaimed Belcher.

"Yes — pre-prohibition wine, pre-San Francisco earthquake wine. I've saved several bottles for special occasions. It's perfectly legal, as you know. Have some!"

This posed an ethical problem for Prohibition Agent Belcher. He was supposed not to partake of the damning beverage. He was supposed to set an example of virtuous non-consumption of the illicit liquid. But he had enjoyed his little tipples on the side at times. Here was a private opportunity — who would know? Pre-prohibition wine. Perfectly legit. He felt a little disgruntled in general from his unpopular line of work. He could use a little pick-me-up. Yes, he definitely need a lift. "I have asthma. I feel a little stuffy. Just a little snort," he acquiesced. "Only because it is pre-prohibition, as you confirm."

Laura hid her face behind another plate. Bobolo nodded and disappeared. He was gone for just a few minutes. From his wine-cellar he selected a bottle of his strongest muscatel. He reentered the kitchen, interrupting small talk between Belcher and Laura while Fiammella kept busy, and sat down at a small table, motioning to Belcher to do the same. Bobolo poured two glasses of muscatel. Belcher gave Laura an unexpected wink in a strange attempt to flirt. Laura was merely amused, being quite experienced with handling guests in such social situations.

"Here you are, Belcher!" said Bobolo, pushing the wine glass towards him with a flourish.

"I w-w-wonder if I sh-sh-should ..." murmured Belcher, lifting his glass to his protruding lips.

"Of course you should. Just a little pepper-upper before you go."

"But I'm not g-g-g-going yet. I haven't inv-v-v-vestigated half the place yet."

"Well, this will strengthen you for the rest of your investigation! Here's to you, Belcher! And here's to wine! May it outlive all governments, all investigations and all damned Prohibition Agents!"

Belcher downed the muscatel in one big gulp before the thrust of Bobolo's strong toast dawned on him *post facto*. He set down the glass and said weakly, "C-c-come, Bónomo, I shouldn't drink to that."

"Here, another. It's one of my best wines." Bobolo re-filled his glass.

Belcher swigged it down, not knowing that one is supposed just to sip muscatel because of its strength, being a wine fortified with additional alcohol such as brandy. "Damned good wine. Yes, d-d-damned good. Now I m-m-must get going on this inv-v-v-vestigation."

"Have another glass," Bobolo insisted and Laura looked at him shyly.

"Just half, j-j-just half a glass. You sure this is p-p-pre-prohibition wine?"

"They've been making it for a thousand years," said Bobolo.

This seemed to satisfy Belcher. He downed another glass quickly, splashing some of it on his vest and necktie. Then he started to get up. Fiammella and Laura watched in amazement as he tried once, twice, three times to get up, each time sinking back into his chair as if pushed down by a giant unseen hand. Finally Bobolo got his hands under Belcher's arms and helped him up.

"Now, if you will es-s-s-scort me around the rest of your place," suggested Belcher.

"Certainly." Bobolo took him by the elbow and led the stumbling Belcher around the yard. While wobbling down the path, Belcher only glanced briefly at a couple of the guest houses. The procession made a humorous pantomime for the bocce players in the yard.

Bobolo was by now pretty sure that he could guide Belcher past his chamber of happiness and its attached winery without the agent even being aware of the cellar. For this purpose he kept up a distracting chatter about guns and hunting until he discovered that prohibition agents had to go about their business unarmed, leaving to officers of the law the more aggressive part of Prohibition such as destruction of barrels and stills. Now, Bobolo decided he'd better distract Belcher's attention from the outside world to the inside world of himself, since they were approaching the door of the dangerous chamber of wine and fellowship.

"Married, Belcher?"

"Yeah. Got a p-p-pretty wife, as wives come ..."

"And go," suggested Bobolo.

"Yeah, that's a g-g-good one!"

"Any children?"

"Yeah, just n-n-now ... one after being married for f-f-fifteen years. Trouble is, the w-w-wife can't n-n-nurse the kid. She's got inverted n-n-nipples. They go in instead of out." By way of demonstration, he plucked at his own bosom while Bobolo stifled a big smile as he held Belcher up.

They were just passing the door of Bobolo's chamber when, twilight having deepened, Beatrice suddenly turned on the entrance light and stood revealed under it.

"L-l-let's go in here," said Belcher.

"Nothing there! Just my daughter."

"Another pretty one. But I w-w-want to take a look."

Bobolo opened the door and gave Beatrice a wink. There, in front of the storeroom wine cellar sat Diana, as per orders, up on her forelegs, a bloodhound Cerberus on guard. Belcher did not yet notice the dog. He saw only the attractive girl.

"H-h-how do you do, young lady?" Belcher tried to make the gesture of tipping a non-existent hat. He succeeded only in tipping himself towards the table, to which he attempted to cling while Bobolo still supported him.

"How do *you* do?" answered Beatrice, suppressing her smile.

"My daughter, Beatrice; Beatrice, this is Mr. Belcher, a very distinguished representative of the United States Government who is assisting in the prohibiting of all festive health-giving, vitamin-rich liquids. He is anti-grapes, you see." Beatrice jammed her handkerchief into her mouth to suppress a giggle. She gave her father a look.

"We just came in to say how-do-you-do," Bobolo said, "and to be sure you are not drinking any forbidden beverage in secret. Now we are going away."

"N-n-not so f-f-fast, Mr. Bónomo. I need to s-s-see more."

"Come, Belcher, we're going now," Bobolo declared and lifted him back from his slanted position against the table.

Belcher felt Bobolo was pushing him too hard. "Damn your interf-f-ference, Bónomo; wait a minute. What's that d-d-door?" Apparently he *still* didn't see the dog. "I think I s-s-smell wine."

"Of course! The wine of your breath!" pointed out Bobolo firmly.

"M-m-mebbe it is and m-m-mebbe it isn't." Belcher lunged out of Bobolo's grasp towards the door … and the dog.

Bobolo let out the hunting cry to which Diana always responded with great leaps and sprintings towards the prey: "*Alla caccia* (To the chase)! *Alla caccia*, Diana!"

Diana responded as to a stag. She leaped up and jumped at Belcher, bowling him over. She stood upon him growling, her incisors bared.

The man screamed. The scream of a man is much more poignant, more soul-rending than the scream of a woman. The whole hilltop was alerted. "S-s-s-save me! Save me!" cried Belcher.

Bobolo was muttering encouragements in Italian to Diana, who was growling like a tiger about to make mincemeat of poor

Belcher. Beatrice contorted in laughter. "If I save you from my bloodhound, will you leave my place and stop bothering me forever, you and your fellow-agents? Forever?"

"Anything, anything you ask, Mr. B-B-Bónomo. Only s-s-save my life from this horrible m-m-monster!" Diana's growls had reached a crescendo, fearsome to hear.

"*Ebbene*, Diana. *Basta, basta* (Very well, Diana. Enough, enough)! Bobolo took his huntress by the collar and she moved her legs one by one off the prostrate man. Gradually her growls diminished like thunder beyond the horizon.

Then Bobolo lifted up the white-faced agent as one would a scarecrow. Belcher flopped across the table. "I n-n-need a swig of something st-st-stronger than wine ..." murmured Belcher.

Bobolo poured a small glass of rum and Belcher swallowed it in three gulps. "Now I'd b-b-better be going home," he said.

"*Una buonissimo* idea," declared Bonomo. He and Beatrice helped Belcher up and guided him out of the door into the yard where a small crowd of guests had collected to enjoy the evening's entertainment.

"Nobody's been killed yet?" called out one of the bocce group, smiling broadly.

"No. Only attempted murder of all pleasure by this government agent," announced Bobolo emphatically, "but now the American people have spoken and all will be well."

Diana the loyal bloodhound leaped out of the door after them and was bounding alongside Belcher as if she wanted nothing more than to knock him down again and sink her teeth into him.

"For G-G-God's sake," cried Belcher, wrenching himself loose from Bobolo's grasp. "C-C-Call off that b-b-bloody b-b-bastard b-b-bitch!"

Belcher began to run and sway, run and sway, as one runs in a nightmare. The onlookers crowed at the sight. Belcher staggered out of the gate, Diana behind him, nipping at his heels. In a few seconds, the faint chirr of Belcher's car could be heard, taking him back to his world of prohibitions.

"And that's the last scene of tonight's play," declaimed Bobolo, bowing low to his guests gathered in the yard. "We shall call this little drama 'Prohibiting Prohibition,' or 'How to Run Off a Drunken Temperance Agent From One's Vineyards.' Now let's have some wine on the house and give a toast to Congress for showing such exalted Solomonic Wisdom in the absurd laws it passes!"

Chapter 15

AMOROUS GLEAM

By 1925 the Bonomo Country Inn was thriving as merrily as a county fair. Four more guest houses had gone up and Mama and the daughters — Beatrice now twenty-seven and Laura twenty-five — had both chosen to stay and work in the family hospitality business. They were all kept busy from morning 'til night making their many customers happy. Papa and Sandro, too, had their hands full maintaining the various structures and keeping the vineyards and gardens producing. Truckloads of supplies streamed up the hill from San Francisco and from towns in the valleys below. In fact Bobolo had been working so hard that he was ready for a vacation. It was about time to go back to Italy for a visit. He announced that he would be leaving on his trip in the fall.

The only one of his friends whom he was able to persuade to accompany him was Serafino Pipitone, who was now quite free, his shy, devoted but rather cold wife having died several years before. Serafino had invented so many useful gadgets for his garage job that he had finally been taken into partnership by the two garage owners, and he was making more money than he really needed. He decided to take four months off and accompany his friend on the jaunt.

Bobolo bought tickets on an Italian ship, the *Palasciano*, but only as far as Lisbon, for he had decided that it was time to see more of Europe. Portugal, Spain, France, Germany and Switzerland were now also on the agenda before visiting his native Italy.

In San Francisco he ordered four new suits and three new hats, and even splurged on a sumptuous gold-headed cane as the ultimate emblem of success. The expedition seemed to his family extravagant and unnecessary. They teased and objected but it made no difference to debonair, determined Bobolo.

"He has no conscience. The devil will catch him yet!" proclaimed Fiammella, without as much heat in her vehemence as in yesteryear.

"Gente allegra Dio l'aiuta (God helps happy people)," countered Bobolo.

"Why do you waste your money, Papa, the minute you've made it?" asked Beatrice.

"People who hide their money away in the darkness are fools. Money is meant to be spent, used, enjoyed. Gold must be out in the sunlight to shine! Life is a fiddle to be played, my daughter. Life is a flask of wine to be savored and absorbed!"

"Life is a pot to be stirred," said Mama, deadpan.

"Why don't you take Mama with you?" Laura suggested.

"Mama? Mama doesn't want to go to Italy! She wants to stay right here and look after the place. She is excellent at what she does and has no desire to leave our hilarity hill where she is so much appreciated as Chef and Hostess."

Mama continued to stir the pot without looking up.

Serafino had to provide himself not only with new suits and hats and shirts but also with a supply of glass eyes sufficient for any losses or accidents on the journey. Bobolo went with him to the small laboratory-shop of the best maker of artificial eyes in the West, Herr Steudel on Market Street in San Francisco.

Herr Steudel was a craftsman from Wiesbaden, a noted glass eye center in Europe. He took his work very seriously, with all of the meticulous solemnity of a German precisionist. His heavy lips hefted a bulky straw-colored mustache; his large blue eyes looked unamused through their spectacles only at what was right before them.

Herr Steudel had just finished comparing again the hues and shadings of Serafino's real eye with the colors and shadings of a tray full of glass eyes when Bobolo said in a most earnest tone, "Herr Steudel, my friend has failed to tell you of a most important circumstance which must be factored into his supply of glass eyes. We are on our way to Paris and Serafino has been single for several years, so my friend needs a very *special* kind of glass eye."

Herr Steudel pushed his spectacles up on his furrowed forehead. "A very spess-i-al kind of glass eye? Why spess-i-al?"

"Ach, Herr Steudel, because one must speak a *very* special language in Paris. The glass eye must amplify the language of desire, of invitation, of passion, of seduction — the language, Herr Steudel, of love. It is very important that you put into my friend's glass eye — an *amorous gleam*."

"An am-orrrous gleam? Wass ist dass? Dass ist a ve-ry un-oo-sual request. I haf never in my life before had such an un-oo-sual request." He put his hand to his brow and pressed his plump fingers into the flesh over his right eyebrow as if to reach deeper levels of thinking.

Bobolo, as usual, was having a lark and could hardly mask his amusement. He winked at Serafino, who was never quite at ease with Bobolo's shenanigans, having been a victim of Bobolo's "fun" too often, as in the keenly remembered ghost episode. He did not, at this moment, know whether to be annoyed at Bobolo's interference in his serious eye-replenishing task or to be a trifle amused. Bobolo himself was enjoying the perplexities of both men.

"But it's a most r-r-r-reasonable r-r-r-request!" intoned Bobolo, rolling his r's in an exaggerated Italian manner. "Most r-r-r-reasonable. Who could think of entering Paris — Paris the beautiful, the alluring, the romantic mistress of the world — with fish eyes, cold, staring, flat, uninviting, unprovocative, expressionless, passionless? No, no, my talented Herr Steudel. My friend Serafino Pipitone is requesting from you — an absolutely unmistakable *amorous gleam* … to attract the ladies immediately into his boudoir!"

"But how, how?" asked Herr Steudel, his bafflement like a casing of Schweitzer cheese all around him. "How can one technically man-oo-facture an amor-r-rous gleam? I haf been making glass eyes of all colors, all sizes, all shapes, all patterns for forty years, but ne-ver an amor-r-r-rous gleam!"

"You are a very great craftsman, Herr Steudel. It can be done. It *must* be done. Anything can be done. Don't tell me that you, with all your technical skill, couldn't make a furious eye or an eye as crafty as a fox, or the gentle eye of an elephant mother. You are the Master of Eyes. All that we are asking you to do is simply to create an eye that allures, invites, tempts — a wayward eye that says powerfully: 'Come into my arms, *Mademoiselle!*'"

In the moment, like a flash of light piercing the darkness, Herr Steudel understood that Bobolo was playing a joke on him and Serafino just to rattle them. Strange people, these Italians. In the days of the Roman Empire, they must have been more serious and clever ... but they have deteriorated so much since then. Probably from having to drink their own wine for two thousand years rather than fine German beer! He decided to go along with Bobolo's jesting ... "But, but are you shu-er, very shu-er that ex-bress-ion r-r-r-resides in the *ball* of the eye, Herr Bon-omo? I am not so shu-er. Let - me - see. Let me look at you, Mr. Pipitone."

Herr Steudel got up and came so close to Serafino that his cheesy breath almost overpowered his customer. Pulling his spectacles from his forehead, Herr Steudel minutely examined Pipitone's optical apparatus. "As I look at you and your ex-bress-ion Mr. Pipitone, ze amor-ous gleam iss not in the cornea, iss not in the iris, iss not in the retina, iss not in the lens. You haf a very distinct ex-bress-ion in this, your good eye, not only from a very high inventive intelligence but also a definite, highly developed amor-ous gleam. This will serve you ver-ie well in Paris ... I lived there once for an entire year when I was young and single. You don't need ze amorous gleam in *both* eyes — just one will do ver-y well with those ver-y amorous, eager, cooperative ladies of Paris! I guarantee it, Serafino! If I am wrong, I will treat you to three days at the Munich Beer Festival during Oktoberfest! And I'm sure you see, Serafino, that Monsieur Bobolo has been jesting ver-y happily with us for the last ten minutes with the amor-ous gleam in *both* his eyes! He is a ver-y naughty, scheming man!"

The tips of Bobolo's red mustache began to quiver as he realized that the emotionally-constricted German had blown his cover! His lips parted to let the breath of laughter through and he began loudly guffawing. The somewhat plump Herr Steudel, perhaps remembering happily his brief flaming youth in Paris, began also to laugh in a rusty way.

Serafino was a little slow to react but then he too began to laugh most freely! He had been about to grab the spare glass eye in his pocket and hurl it at Herr Steudel's tray of glass eyes.

When Bobolo stopped laughing he said, "Three cheers for you, Herr Steudel, you jolly, sausage-and-cheese-eating Kraut! You got the last laugh on me, which is wonderful. It doesn't happen very often but I am learning to get full enjoyment out of such situations when they occur! It's good for my Florentine soul and I am delighted when any clever colleague-in-humor wins. The more laughter-loving people there are, the happier the world! You will have to change the name on your store to 'Steudel's Glass Eyes and Laughter!'"

Chapter 16

MUSSOLINI VISITS THE INN

Bobolo was gone for four months. Presumably he enjoyed his travels through Europe in late 1925 but how was one to know? He never shared contemporaneous accounts of his trip with any member of his family. One of the joys of travel, he believed, was the sense of freedom it proffered, not restricted by any ties with home. His family knew he would regale them later with tales of his trip, suitably enhanced with the embellishments of time.

He and Serafino had separated on reaching Florence, Bobolo to remain in his native city, Pipitone to proceed to his original home site of Naples, the birthplace of pizza.

Bobolo had gotten into trouble almost immediately with Mussolini's Fascist authorities who had taken over the government in early 1925 and ruled it thereafter as a one-party state. Bobolo was filled with a natural independence, upon which was superimposed his tremendous admiration for the Risorgimento liberators of Italy. Because he esteemed all fighters for independence and the great traditions of freedom of his adopted country of America, he loathed the sight of every symbol and manifestation of Fascism.

Bobolo spoke frankly, exactly as he thought, wherever he went. He insulted the Fascist officers of Customs, of the city, of the local police force. He thumbed his nose both verbally and digitally, with an extended finger in his pocket if not in the open. It was all that the American Consul in Florence could do to keep bailing him out of his successive troubles. But Bobolo enjoyed every moment of his one-man rebellion. The Consul gave a great sigh of relief when Bobolo at last headed for Naples and the steamship to New York.

In Florence a throng of relatives saw him off at the train station and helped him with the innumerable boxes and bags he had accumulated. He had spent with a lavish hand. He had given generous monetary gifts to all his relatives in Italy and had purchased many gifts for his family and friends in California. He had acquired several amusing Swiss musical contraptions for the house, among them a hat-rack that played a tune when hat or coat was hung upon it and a toilet seat which sang out the lyric from Donizetti's *L'Elisir d'Amore* when sat upon. He had purchased several marble statuettes for the garden … and, strangely, he acquired a large painted terra-cotta bust of Mussolini.

His family was overjoyed to see Bobolo when he returned home in late January 1926. Mama had worked even harder in his absence and was basically resentful of the whole trip, including that Bobolo never entertained a thought of asking her along. She welcomed him back, not as if he were devil incarnate but as if he were the Angel Gabriel. She had paid some attention to Father Simeone's confessional advice.

Bobolo had a wonderful time placing the marble statues in the garden. Only the terra-cotta bust of Mussolini seemed out of place.

"I do not see the logic. Why would you buy this?" complained Fiammella. "You hate Mussolini as if he were ten thousand devils and yet you put up a statue of him in the garden. *Non capisco.* I don't understand."

"You will see! You will see!" replied Bobolo. "Never judge a man before his purposes are fulfilled."

Bobolo proceeded to make a low, six inch fluted pedestal, like the pedestal of a lamp post, and set the bust atop it, close to the ground on the garden pathway called *Via della Libertá* (Liberty Way).

When his friends came to their first regular Saturday supper meeting after the statue was set in place, they too protested.

"Mussolini? Why Mussolini when you say you love liberty above all things. Did the dictator win you over on your trip? *Vergogna!* For shame, Bobolo."

"Wait, my friends. Suspend your judgment. If I have not fully justified Mussolini's place in my garden a month from this evening, I give you permission to bring your sledgehammers and destroy it before my very eyes!"

"Very well, very well! But you do surprise us, Bobolo!"

"Surprise, my friends, is the end of boredom and the beginning of fun."

A month later Bobolo waited at the front gate. When all his friends had arrived, he conducted them to *Via della Libertá* and said, "Now is the time for us to check up on our wager, to visit my Mussolini statue." When they all stood around the bust, Bobolo instructed, "Wait here, my friends."

He went to his guest house chamber, opened the door and released Diana. She loped directly and easily towards the statue of Mussolini. Bobolo leaned down, stroked Diana on her hindquarters and asked, *"Comé si da un bere a Mussolini, Diana* (How does one give a drink to Mussolini, Diana)?" Diana lifted a hind leg and squirted bountifully on the painted face of Benito, the Fascist tyrant. The assembled friends roared with laughter.

Then Bobolo released Leo from the wine cellar. Leo loped directly to the painted effigy and duplicated the saturation of urine on Mussolini's face. Bobolo's friends were slapping their thighs and clapping one another's shoulders with delight.

"Now, my friends, do you understand?" asked Bobolo.

"Now we understand — *bravo, bravissimo*! You win the wager, Bobolo!"

Bobolo tipped his imaginary hat, bowed and said, "My faithful dogs have demonstrated how we feel about Mussolini! Come back in a month and you will see even more impressive testimony of how they feel about this demagogue ruler of Italy.

Chapter 17

QUIET HAPPINESS

It was a lovely late March afternoon in 1927. Bobolo had finished early what he considered to be an adequate number of chores for the day, although he and Sandro could well occupy themselves from the time the sun rose over the hills to the time it left its last glimmer in the evening.

Bobolo relished late afternoons like this to think, to daydream, to savor simple pleasures like the breeze and the view. He had moved from bench to bench, following the sun. Now he reached the bench outside his chamber door. From here he could view all of his domain, from the gentle hills sloping north towards far-away San Francisco to the near hills and valleys of San Jose.

The grasses of the hills had turned green with the spring rains and there were glints of interspersed golden poppies, yellow acacia and sea-blue lupin. The scattered live oak trees with their rough gray trunks and branches, their dark green clumped foliage, gave the unmistakable accent of California.

On the terrace below him, two plum trees in bloom shed their blossoms gently, like white moths fluttering slowly to the ground. Near the dining room window a tangerine tree still held its perennial crop of orange fruit. And of course he always derived great pleasure from gazing at his stately Italian cypress trees uplifting their tall, narrow, dark green shapes so uniquely into the sky.

On the whole, it was a good world or, at least, there were good things in it … glimpses of affection, abundant evidence of friendship, gusts of laughter, glasses of good wine, platters of spaghetti, mountains with red-tailed hawks soaring above, and deer cavorting among the live oak. There was ample sunshine and time like this for silent reflection.

There were still evil things, too, and disagreeable. He hoped that there would be no bickering and no scolding in that Heaven in which he did not believe. If only there could be perfect peace in families and brotherhood among the families of nations.

If only his family could love him as he loved them. Perhaps they had their moments of loving him but the intermittent tone always seemed to be of disapproval. How little they understood him and his dreams ... How immensely good the sunlight was ... the most perfect of all essences. All he wanted was peace and warm, life-giving sunshine.

A call of reproof came through his sleep. It was the voice of Beatrice, now twenty-nine years old, unmarried as yet and still learning the restaurant and hotel management business from her mother. Although she had admirers, she was too busy to pay sufficient attention to them to keep them attracted.

"Papa! You were supposed to go down to the village to get some supplies for Mama. Don't you remember? And now it's too late. All the shops are closed. What are you doing here, dreaming?"

"Dreaming? Yes, the greatest luxury in the world ... health-giving sleep and mind-activating dreams."

"Oh, Papa! How could you sleep? Why don't you work more? Why don't you stick to things and make more money, like Mr. Giannini? You're as smart at he is and more likable. He's worth millions, one of the greatest bankers in the world!"

Bobolo knew from what source those words derived! "Ah, my child, if you could but learn a basic lesson of life, better than all the schoolbook lessons you ever learned, even in Junior College, the essential truth of the old saying, *'chi si accontenta gode'* — a contented mind is a perpetual feast. Which means that he who knows how to content himself knows the very secret of happiness."

Chapter 18

PRIDE OF ITALY

Amedeo Bruni and his guest entered Bobolo's yard at the Bonomo Country Inn at an inauspicious moment. On that Sunday afternoon in mid-May 1928, Bobolo was, as usual of late, dozing and dreaming in the sun, his two dogs, Pinocchio and Diana the Second, lying affectionately at his feet. He had fallen asleep thinking of his friends who would be coming down for Saturday evening supper, and of the beauty of friendship lasting for decades.

He had forgotten that Fiammella had asked him to gather some heads of lettuce from the garden and to clean and fill the wine flasks at the tables. She herself had been sudsing dish cloths in the dishpan. Stepping out of the kitchen door to hang up the cloths, she beheld her worthless spouse dozing in the sun. It did something to her. It set the fiery wheel revolving inside of her which nowadays she usually tried hard to suppress. Sometimes she just couldn't. She wrung and flung the dish cloths over the line, went back into the kitchen, took the pan of warm soapy water from the sink, strode across the room with it, out the kitchen door and across the yard to the bench where her Lord and Master lay dreaming, doing nothing. Without hesitation she flung the dishpan full of soapy water over Bobolo's face, head, shoulders and unresisting body. "Take that, *pigraccio-accio-accio* (most, most lazy one)! *Fanullone!* (Loafer)!"

A sopping Bobolo rose with feigned dignity and started to protest but stopped quickly because of soapy water streaming into his mouth from his head.

There was a burst of men's laughter from the edge of the yard. Bobolo, rubbing soap from his eyes, was just able to make out the figure of Amedeo Bruni, the famous vineyardist, and a tall man standing beside him. Both were convulsed with laughter, especially Amedeo, whose body was swaying with successive waves of hilarity.

"A fine kettle of fish!" spat Bobolo to a departing Fiammella when the drenching left him able to talk. "A woman should keep to her kitchen and leave a man to his dreams. Don't you know it's work to dream such dreams as I have? And now you've disgraced yourself, not me, before Amedeo Bruni and his friend."

Bobolo tried to smooth out his soapy hair and mustache and to pull his shirt and trousers into shape. Then he crossed the yard towards his guests, feeling like a wet dog but smiling as broadly as if nothing untoward had happened.

Fiammella had disappeared into into the kitchen. She was already in the depths of remorse and self-pity. Why had she done such a thing? And, Holy Madonna, why did some fine person always have to turn up to witness such scenes, from which Bobolo always managed to emerge as the damaged saint and she as the damaging sinner? Bobolo would be requiring an extra fine supper for Bruni and his guest plus the other friends who would be dropping by and, as usual, she wouldn't be getting a mite of help out of him. She set to work cleaning the wine flasks he had neglected.

Bobolo, dripping, rushed towards his old friend. "Ah, Bruni! I welcome you and your friend with overflowing hospitality! My wife insisted I be freshly clean to greet you! *Vieni! Vieni* (Come! Come)! We will have a fine supper and good talk!"

"My undaunted, un-submergible friend! It is great to see you! Let me present my good friend, Gelasio Teano."

"Gelasio! My wet hand! Any friend of Amedeo is always welcome at Casa Bonomo."

"Thank you, Bonomo! That is indeed an impressive welcome."

They laughed, Bruni more easily than Gelasio. There was something a little self-conscious, a little over-dignified about Gelasio. He was a tall, well-made man with a distinguished Roman face and the linguistic accent of modern Rome. Bobolo couldn't quite pigeon-hole him.

Bruni was always entertaining celebrities at his unusual home in Sonoma Valley which was a replica of the newly discovered House of the Vetii at Pompeii, with its low-lying rooms and beautiful deep red-backgrounded frescoes. Yet this guest of Bruni's was not dressed like a celebrity; he wore a checked shirt open at the neck and old blue denim trousers.

"You are Roman by your accent," surmised Bobolo.

"Yes, I'm on my way home to Rome after a visit to your beautiful California. I would like to see more of your place before it gets dark, Signor Bonomo, if I may. Bruni tells me it is a fine Italian estate of California."

Bobolo's face lighted happily, for he was exceedingly proud of his domain. They started out along the paths of the upper terrace where Gelasio stooped to see the broken bits of dolls and wheels and china, the fragments of childhood and the family embedded in the cement walks and steps everywhere.

"*Una brava idea!* A charming idea," he said. "You are a man of feeling, Bonomo. *Bravo il sentimento!*"

"Ah, no, to the devil with sentiment!" exclaimed Bobolo. "Step on it as we are stepping now. What is love in the end but a dishpan of soapy water?"

The two men looked to see how serious might be the expression of Bobolo's face. He allowed a merry twitch of his red mustache but his eyes were without twinkle.

They arrived shortly at *Via della Libertá*, with the bust of Mussolini at its entrance. "Ah, bravo!" said Gelasio. "His

Excellency, Benito Mussolini." Bobolo was a little surprised at the admiration and enthusiasm in Gelasio's voice.

"As we all know, humor may come at the expense of those in politics, especially if they are rising in power," warned Bobolo. He lifted his voice and called out "Pinocchio! Pinocchio!"

Pinocchio, who had been barking at a squirrel in a live oak tree, came loping. "Pinocchio, *comé si da a bere a Mussolini?*" asked Bobolo. Pinocchio turned, trotted to the statue, lifted a leg and gave Mussolini his drink.

Bruni didn't restrain his laughter. Gelasio smiled broadly, but his face flushed. He nodded his head to acknowledge the wit but didn't seem pleased with the target.

They moved on down the hill. Bobolo exhibited his dining hall, guest houses, hard clay bocce court, the stable, enlarged vegetable garden, orchard of fruit trees, their large ten year-old olive grove and the lovely vineyard spreading down the hill. Ubiquitous white grape blossoms were emerging promisingly from the vines. The tall cypress trees were duly noted.

"These hills remind me of the Alban hills south of Rome, which many don't know have a volcanic origin, now concealed by time," said Gelasio.

"As they remind me of the Tuscan hills around Florence," said Bobolo. "They are all brother hills." Gelasio flashed a look of quiet admiration at Bobolo, almost as to a poet.

By the time they came round to Bobolo's private Chamber of Mirth, Angelo and Serafino were arriving with Passerino who had journeyed down from the city on the six o'clock train. There were introductions and the three newcomers seemed to be taken more or less comfortably into the group although there may have been a slight air of constraint. Amedeo Bruni was a very rich man who, though still amiable, thought of himself on a golden plateau above many of his fellow Italians in California. Gelasio was an unknown, a somewhat distant but dignified man who was clearly making a great effort to be amicable.

They all moved into Bobolo's chamber and he immediately brought out a fine California sherry. They sat talking and sipping their aromatic drinks in the sunset-lighted room with doors and windows open, while the beautiful hills beyond the vineyard glowed through all the progressive tints of a typical Italian backdrop at sunset.

"It's a kind of *paradiso*, California," said Gelasio. "No wonder everyone speaks of this state as *'la bella, bella* California.' If I ever become disenchanted with Rome or its leadership, I would willingly move to your lovely environs in this region of California."

Bobolo replied, "Perhaps you should be ready to pack, Gelasio. I studied history as well as literature during my years at the University of Florence and I see trends in today's politics in Italy which could become alarming in the future. Do you see such a drift in governmental speech and legislation coming out of Rome which suggest leanings towards Caesarism in the future?"

In a quiet voice, Gelasio responded. "If one studies the development and rule of the Roman Empire, the Caesars provided us with some of the most durable and enlightened administrations in a thousand years. Similarly to the Ancient Persians. Dukedoms and principalities of the Middle Ages, including hundreds of years of well-informed rule in Venice, led Europe into the Renaissance, triggering a great flowering of beauty and scintillating arts. Don't you agree, Bobolo?"

At this point, thirty-two year old Beatrice, a handsome young lady sporting an appealing smile, brought in a large platter of ravioli swimming in an aromatic chestnut brown sauce. The conversation paused while the table was pushed into the center of the room. As the men redistributed themselves around the table, Beatrice passed out utensils and lovely Italian cypress-decorated linen napkins. To each gentleman, she served a generous portion of Fiammella's special ravioli, a favorite recipe from Firenze.

As they began to dine, Bobolo responded to Gelasio's question. "Yes, your points are well made. There are certainly magnificent legacies from Ancient Persia, the Roman Empire and Western

Civilization's Renaissance — who could argue that? But there are also vivid examples in the past few hundred years of inevitable drifts towards unlimited power and dictatorship, no matter what the ruler is called, which have quashed any semblance of individual liberty and happiness and have destroyed millions of lives. Could that be happening now in Italy and Germany, for instance?"

Gelasio was impressed by Bobolo's words and warnings, almost professorial, yet coming from a grape grower, innkeeper and noted local prankster from hills overlooking the small farming town of San Jose. "My dear Bonomo, Mussolini has already accomplished some remarkable things. Italy was in bad shape economically after World War I, even though they switched sides away from Germany in the last year of the war. Italy was ready for the wolves, the communists and every other evil social force. He took it and fastened it together, welded and strengthened it so that all classes benefitted. He has made mistakes, but what leader hasn't?"

"I don't see a great leader in Mussolini," said Bobolo. "He seems more pompous than real, almost trying to emulate a Roman Emperor without the educational or political background to establish any credentials. He finished high school but was booted out of the University of Lausanne for his disruptive radical ideas. He continued expressing various extreme viewpoints as a newspaper writer, then went directly into politics in his twenties when the opportunity opened up because of post-war chaos in Germany and Italy. I see absolutely no resemblance to Augustus, Trajan, Hadrian, Marcus Aurelius or Constantine. Tell me, do you?"

"Bonomo," interjected Gelasio in his quiet dignified voice, wiping tasty ravioli sauce from his lips, "I've lived in Rome all my life and I've watched the fortunes of my country with passionate interest. I'm convinced that Mussolini has done far more good than harm to Italy. He's strengthened our country politically, economically, militarily — in every way. He is no fool; far from it. You must give him a chance, Bonomo." He paused, took a sip of sherry, then continued in his distinguished, refined Roman accent, "The people trust him, the nobility trust him and the King trusts him."

At this point, Amedeo Bruni wisely thought that the discussion of Italian politics had run their course. "Let's change the subject, friend Bobolo," he suggested. "Gelasio's grandfather was a great student and lover of Dante and I've told Gelasio how well you love your Dante, your Virgil, your Petrarch — and even Boccaccio."

"Amedeo mentions a trio of great Italian poets," replied Bobolo. He then signaled to Beatrice, who had just returned to the room, to refill their wine glasses with the wine of the night, a special 1920 Cabernet Sauvignon from their vineyard. "Of course one finds Dante 'under the sun and under the stars' in *tutto il mondo*, everywhere. But here, on these California hills, I'm even more often reminded of Virgil and his *Georgics* of 29 BC. My vineyard, my olive-trees, the passing of sun and stars and weather over my fields, all speak to me of Virgil ..." Bobolo began to quote in Latin some rhymed lines from the *Georgics*:

> "What makes the cornfields rejoice; under what star it is well to turn the brown earth ... of this will I sing, O Maecenas ...

> "And now of thee, Bacchus, will I sing, Lord of the Grapes!
> The juice foams — come, Lord of the Grapes, take off thy boots and stain thy bared feet in the red juice ...

> "While Caesar wages mighty war, I walk the flowering ways of quietness ..."

"Bravo, bravissimo, Signor Bobolo!" said Gelasio. "You are bringing me to unexpected tears in your idyllic California paradise. He who loves what Virgil loves is a contented man."

The evening went on well and peacefully after that special Virgilian moment. Great platters of *piccione con polenta* (squab and cornmeal) and artichokes stuffed with mildly-salted anchovies were borne in and taken away empty by Beatrice and Laura, who often were pulled into the conversation before they left by questions about themselves. They gave their answers in lovely-accented Florentine, to the delight of all. The cabernet flowed freely but not excessively before being changed to a soft, sweet chardonnay when dessert was brought in, large primavera glasses containing a delicate, foamy chestnut whip flavored with tangerines.

Bobolo had recently been thinking again of introducing, once a month, brief post-prandial entertainment by talented performers. By luck and chance, this evening he had arranged with one of Mimi Imperator's retired tenor opera singers, newly moved from San Francisco to San Jose, to sing just one aria after dinner, then depart in her new fancy car. After they had finished the truly delicious meal, Bobolo invited his guests to move into the inn's main dining hall for a special treat.

The guest performer, Donna Biancamano, began to sing the most famous and beautiful aria from Puccini's *Turandot* — *Nessun Dorma* (Let No One Sleep). The men, whether familiar with it such as Amedeo, Bobolo and Gelasio, or not, such as Serafino, Angelo and Passerino, were brought near tears by her high tenor rendering of the tragic scene from the final act of *Turandot*:

> *Dilegua, o notte!*
> *Tramontate, stelle!*
> *Tramontate, stelle!*
> *All'alba, vincerò*
> *Vincerò! Vincerò!*
>
> Vanish, o night!
> Fade, you stars!
> Fade, you stars!
> At dawn, I will win!
> I will win! I will win!

After the performance, Bobolo suggested sitting outside for a few minutes before returning to their private chamber of happiness, its dining table now cleaned off and leaning on its side against a wall. With his guests now sitting on a sofa and in comfortable chairs, conversation resumed in amicable and lively fashion until 10 PM when Amedeo and Gelasio made the move to leave. After all, it was a Sunday evening and Amedeo didn't want it ending in any wine-inspired conversational over-exuberance. He reminded the group that this was Gelasio's final night of his San Francisco visit, that he was leaving for New York and Italy the next afternoon.

"You have given me a very refreshing and delightful time in the country, Signor Bonomo, and I thank you heartily for it," said Gelasio, rising and extending his hand. "I asked Bruni to select for me a fine typical Italian who had settled in California and had become a good American while still retaining his love for Italy. I wanted to see how such Italians lived, how well they had transplanted. You were a perfect choice. I learned much and will long remember my visit."

"The pleasure was ours," answered Bobolo.

"Bobolo," said Amedeo, "I think it is now time to reveal the identity of your guest. I have played a trick on you. I told Gelasio that you were not only a well-educated, stimulating and interesting person, one of the only philosophers of life in the vineyard business, but also an accomplished prankster, the merriest in California. I also reminded Gelasio that, as Petrarch said in the 1300's in his *Trionfo d'Amore*:

> *Ché chi prende diletto di far frode,*
> *Non si de' lamentar s'altri l'inganna.*

> Those who delight in tricking others
> Shouldn't complain when others trick them.

"My friend Bobolo, you have had the honor of entertaining His Highness, Gelasio Caetani, Count of Fondi, Duke of Sermoneta and of San Marco, the Prince of Teano."

Serafino, Angelo and Passerino stumbled to their feet. Many might be overwhelmed, but Bobolo Bonomo retained his poise, equal to the occasion.

"Prince Caetani, you honor my little California homestead — it's our privilege and pleasure to have you here. We are simple folk. Tonight we have been ourselves, undisguised. You have seen us as we are." Bobolo breathed a quiet sigh of relief to himself. There were times during their conversations about Mussolini that he had wanted to make much more powerful negative comments and criticize Caetani for his apparent admiration of the Fascist leader.

"Exactly why I wanted to meet you, Bobolo. You have been stimulating and delightful. Italy and I are very proud of you."

"I have greatly enjoyed your visit, which was an elegant subterfuge, Amadeo. I completely agree with Petrarch that humorists must not only make others laugh but also genuinely appreciate jokes on themselves." He then let out a loud, reverberating laugh. All those in the room smiled in response.

Chapter 19

FIAMMELLA'S EYRIE

For a month after the embarrassing episode of Fiammella hurling the basin of soapy water onto Bobolo, unwittingly witnessed by Amedeo and the Duke of Fondi, Fiammella retreated into herself and reassessed her life. She continued working hard, threw no insults at Bobolo, and spent a great deal of time alone, walking around the property or just staying in the marital room, mostly by herself.

In mid-June 1928, she asked Bobolo for an important conference in their room. "Bobolo, I need to change my lifestyle. I've been working continuously, seven days a week, for almost twenty-two years. As you know, I am fifty-five years old and I would like to slow down."

"I agree, my dearest Fiammella. You have been an absolute work-horse as Chef and Hostess of our wonderful inn. Perhaps I have been the main idea-person but it is certainly you who have daily made the fine reputation of this place. What's on your mind?"

"As we both know, Beatrice and Laura, after graduating from San Mateo County Community College, each spent six months at The Culinary Institute of Florence, learning far more than I could teach them about the intricacies and delights of Italian cooking and also perfecting their Italian language while living with my family, none of whom speak English."

"Yes, that was your idea and I have always told everyone how brilliant you were not only to create that opportunity for their training but to insist upon it."

"Yes, you have. Now it is past time to start giving them new responsibilities in running and managing our family inn. After all, Beatrice is now thirty-two years old and Laura is thirty."

"What do you have in mind?"

"Beatrice is a natural and creative chef. I want to make her Head Chef soon and pass the kitchen over to her. I want to decrease my role right away, cutting to four days a week from seven and stopping completely in less than a year, only helping on special occasions. Enough is enough."

"Have you discussed this with Beatrice?" asked Bobolo.

"Yes, she likes the idea and is eager to take over. Laura will initially help out in the kitchen but she will gradually assume my management role as hostess, reservations manager, record keeper and financial administrator. She has all of those skills, has a more outgoing personality and will make an excellent hostess. We both know she may marry her long-time boyfriend Marcello one of these days. As you also know, he has a Master's in Business from U.C. Berkeley and would prove invaluable to us. We both hold him in high personal esteem. He is from an Italian family and speaks fluent Italian."

"I like all these ideas ... yes, I do," he said, looking at her. "And what else is on your mind?"

"I have decided we both need more time separately, for ourselves. From my perspective, my frustrations build up and my anger builds up ... and then I explode and do something reckless like throwing a pan of soapy water over you. Somebody almost always witnesses my outbursts which makes me feel stupid and very annoyed at myself."

"What do you suggest?"

"I need my own place, a haven of my very own where I can retreat and be by myself ... completely by myself where no one else can intrude."

"For all of the time or just some of the time?" asked Bobolo, concerned by the implications of what she was saying.

"A retreat for just some of the time, for instance when you are spending happy time with your fellow Angels and ghosts on weekends."

"Specifically, what did you have in mind?"

"My own eyrie — Fiammella's Eyrie!"

"Fiammella's what?"

"I thought you spent two years at the University of Florence studying literature."

"I did but I never came across that word!"

"You never read *Hamlet?*"

"I did, actually, but it was an Italian translation," said Bobolo.

"*Traditore, tradutorre!* The translator is a traitor! Ha! Are you impressed with my scholarly erudition?"

"Yes, I am, indeed! Who was your tutor?" asked Bobolo.

"My friend, Barbara, who majored in English at the University of San Francisco and now lives in San Jose. I spent time with her when you were galavanting around Europe for four months without me. She has a great deal of common sense and helped me gel my ideas while you were playing pranks on Fascists."

"So, what did Shakespeare mean by 'eyrie?'"

"Eagle's nest," replied Fiammella. "A retreat high in the sky, away from everyone else, where one can be alone and feel safe to relax, to gentle one's mind, releasing pent-up emotions and frustrations harmlessly. One can pursue one's hobbies at one's own pace and be contentedly alone!"

"Sounds good to me! My hobbies are people and laughter. Please translate your goals into tangible construction ideas."

"All right. I want my own six-story round tower, built of stone, to be constructed twenty-seven yards east of our marital bedroom just where the hill slopes steeply, so trees can never block my view of the valley or the mountains beyond."

"Why six stories?" asked Bobolo.

"For the best views and to fulfill the definition of an eyrie."

"So what's on each level, my favorite Tuscan architect?"

"The top level will be a lookout with my own small telescope and binoculars," answered Fiammella. "I have become an amateur birder over the years, which you may not know, and I derive great pleasure from the hobby, though I have had little time to pursue it. Also on the sixth floor will be a small pool, my very own, with sunshades and a comfortable lounging chair. Perhaps I will even become a nudist!"

Bonomo refrained from comment. "And on the fifth floor?"

"My bedroom, featuring a wide single bed, with no room for any male! Mine and mine alone, along with a small dining table which can be easily moved towards sunrises or sunsets as I deem appropriate for the best view in accordance with my mood."

"Go on," urged Bobolo. "Your ideas sound very good to me."

"On the fourth floor is to be my artist's studio."

"Your what? Are you going to model for some Bohemian artist, maybe in the nude?"

"No, this is where I will do my painting. You know I have always enjoyed sketching. When you were courting me in Florence, you loved my cartoons. Then while you were in Europe, I took painting lessons from a local artist. Now I want to paint landscapes and perhaps even birds with whatever abilities I have. I enjoy painting; it relaxes my mind."

"And on the other levels of your eagle's nest?" asked Bobolo.

"On the ground floor, an elevator for only one person. Just me! Plus a dumbwaiter system for bringing meals and supplies up to the higher floors."

"And on the second and third floors?"

"Canons, spears, death traps, machine guns, lions, tigers … and whatever else is necessary to keep the male species from ever entering my private eyrie!"

"Ha! Anything else?" asked Bobolo, smiling. He was impressed and proud of her.

"Yes. I want you to hire a certified architect right away. I want my eyrie first class, though not overdone with extravagance. I have decided *not* to demand it be constructed of Michelangelo's white Carrara marble from the famous quarries of Italy. Local rock will do. I am a simple eagle."

Bobolo smiled. And he bowed to his surprising wife.

Chapter 20

TUSCAN HILLS

Fiammella's eyrie was completed in four months, by the end of October 1928, including a hedge-lined flagstone walkway marked "Private" from their marital quarters to the tall stone tower at the edge of the hill.

The new lifestyles of each had a very beneficial effect on both of them. Bobolo never again played pranks on Fiammella and she never again threw soapy or even non-soapy water on him. Her cantankerous nature markedly eased and they each began seeing more and more of each other's strengths and virtues.

Within nine months, Beatrice and a hired sous-chef handled all the meals, with the restaurant closed every Monday except for cafeteria service for the few guests in residence. A shuttle service was provided for those who wanted to have dinner in the now-bourgeoning city of San Jose. Laura and her husband Marcello ran the entire administrative aspects of the business, instituting many cost-saving measures such as bulk buying, investing extra money rather than depositing it in the bank, doubling the size of the vineyards and using more modern equipment and methods of wine-processing.

In 1930, Tranquillino at the age of twenty-seven, with four years of college at Berkeley under his belt, purchased Mimi Imperato's entertainment facility, a combined restaurant and stage, in San Francisco. Before she died, Mimi had made sure in her Will that it be offered to him at a reasonable fixed price. It continued to thrive under his very capable and jovial management.

Fiammella blossomed in her eyrie. She was healthy, smiled more, slept well and painted her landscapes and birds with increasing skill, even selling a few of her paintings displayed in a San Jose gallery. She was working towards an exhibit of her own. She looked content and only rarely lost her temper. A new wife had emerged … and she never let Bobolo into her eagle's nest despite his many and various requests.

She spent four nights a week sharing the marital bed with Bobolo. Both seemed more than content with their new, and sometimes even exciting, compatibility. To celebrate the first anniversary of the inauguration of her eyrie in the sky, in late October of 1929, despite the woes on Wall Street, Bobolo gave a champagne party just for the two of them in their marital suite. He had wanted it to take place in her eyrie but she wouldn't budge. This was the one firm rule for her eyrie — no males allowed.

Over the years, Bobolo had generally forgotten about their wedding night which had been so badly influenced by champagne. The 8 PM party for the two of them consisted only of *hors d'oeuvres* and two bottles of champagne, already opened, with artificial corks put into the bottles, easy to remove. Bobolo handled his champagne well, only sipping. Fiammella, serving herself, lost track despite warnings by Bobolo. They discussed many pleasant things, with Fiammella getting more emotional as the champagne took hold. By 10 PM she began to bring up more subjects which Bobolo couldn't divert despite his best efforts.

"Bobolo, I have had recurrent worries since our wedding night that I said something terrible to you which precipitated your departure into the Greek war. What did I say?"

"Nothing important, my dear. That was long ago and I have forgotten the specifics," replied Bobolo.

"I'm sure you haven't forgotten. You are gifted with an amazing memory. I must've … what did I say?"

"I can't remember. Let's drop the subject," said Bobolo.

"Please. Tell me."

"Whatever you told me has been forgiven or forgotten long ago. Let's talk about something else, like our present great relationship, so much improved by your eyrie."

"Bobolo. I think I shocked you that night. I must have told you …"

"No, Fiammella," he stopped her. "That's a figment of your imagination. You told me nothing important about yourself. If you must know, you did make derogatory remarks about our very quick marital consummation. It was quite embarrassing to me. We Italian men believe we are great lovers. On our first attempt, I wasn't and it was very humiliating. That's all that happened. But it did shake me up; I chose to go to war and let God decide whether I should survive such embarrassment."

"Okay, Bobolo. Although I suspect there was more, I thank you for explaining that, and for your selective memory. I apologize for my role in your quick departure. It was terrible for a bride to embarrass her new husband, whatever I said. You have certainly made it up to me. When we are getting along well, Bobolo, you are an excellent lover!"

"So are you, my dearest eagle. Since you've had your own eyrie, we have been getting better and better with each other, haven't we?"

"We have," responded Fiammella as she guided him to their couch. They slowly took off their clothes and climbed into bed, Bobolo with hopeful anticipation. She turned towards him, put her arm around his side, said, "Sweet dreams, my love," and fell immediately into a lightly-snoring sleep.

Yes, we are truly married, thought Bobolo, and he laughed quietly.

* * *

A year and a half later, on May 16, 1931, Fiammella was lying in the sun next to her sixth floor eyrie pool, thinking of her contented retirement after so many years of hard work and her very pleasant relationship with her husband since she had built her solitary, peaceful eagle's nest.

Bobolo had taken a walk around their property and was now sitting on a bench surveying his vineyard, admiring the view and thinking what a fortunate man he was. He suddenly clutched his painful chest, the pain extending down his left arm. He thought for a moment, then smiled broadly and laughed aloud, as certain ancient Celtic warriors, fatally wounded on the battlefield, used to do when they realized that the end of the Comedy of Life was fast approaching.

After a lifetime of jokes, pranks and mirthful fun, bringing enrichment and happiness to his family and friends, Bobolo Bonomo fell forward and died at the age of fifty-nine in the lovely green Tuscan hills of his California surround.

Afterword

The concept of making something good derive from something bad goes back thousands of years — probably as far back as our earliest human ancestors more than a million years ago. The Bible has many references to the subject. The sixty-first sermon of St. Augustine (354-430) was titled "Ex Malo Bonum," making good come from bad.

Stanford University was founded by Leland and Jane Stanford after the death of their only son, Leland Stanford, Jr. at the age of fifteen from typhoid fever in Italy in 1884. Leland Stanford, Sr., told his wife, "The children of California shall be our children." Stanford University, founded the next year, has yielded profound good from their devastating loss.

The Coronavirus pandemic of 2020-2021 has tragically impacted our entire world. The least affected were those who remained free of the powerful virus but even their lives were impressively changed. Co-editor Cathy Altrocchi Waidyatilleka, a granddaughter of this book's author, Julia Cooley Altrocchi, had her lifestyle and career as a prep school teacher in Honolulu significantly altered. The senior co-editor, Paul Hemenway Altrocchi, younger son of the author, at age 89 had to lead the lifestyle of an isolated monk in his small apartment. He was about to buy yak butter candles and Tibetan prayer books when Cathy, also living in Honolulu, handed him the Bobolo manuscript and suggested he review it as a possible pandemic project to forestall full-fledged candle-lit, chanting Monk-hood.

Paul had inherited the Bobolo manuscript in 1972 but transferred it to Cathy when he moved from the mainland to

Hawaii in 2000. When Cathy showed him the manuscript as a possible pandemic project in early 2020, he re-read it and loved it. He asked Cathy to read it and she loved it too, so they decided to co-edit the book as a Corona Virus Epidemic Endeavor — no masks required! Something good to derive from something bad.

Author Julia began writing the book in the summer of 1953. Her manuscript was rejected by two major publishers in 1955 and 1956. She moved on to other projects and did not revise the manuscript further.

Julia was not a comedic writer nor a joking person in her early or mid-adult life. She was originally a poet, publishing her first book of poetry, *The Poems of A Child*, when she was eleven. She had a distinguished lifelong career as a poet, historian and writer of historical novels, receiving numerous awards. She was twice President of the prestigious California Writers Club.

As a member of Vassar's Class of 1914, she was a shy introvert who apparently spent much of her time gazing at the moon, contemplating the meaning of life and the universe, and writing poetry — a strategy not designed to be voted "Most Popular" in one's class. She made a few close friends but was little known to most of her classmates. Yet in 1964, at her fiftieth reunion in Poughkeepsie, she regaled her classmates for four days with a veritable tsunami of well-told funny anecdotes and stories and was voted "Most Changed" in her class. What caused such an impressive personality change?

Firstly, she discovered, at age forty-seven, that she was part Irish. This family secret was kept from her until that time because of strong anti-Irish sentiment in New England in the second half of the 19th Century (see *Venom and Laughter* by Julia Cooley Altrocchi, published in 2012), and because of powerful anti-Irish sentiment within her own family by descendants of second-son English immigrants to America who had been taught to detest the peasant Irish settlers in the USA.

At age forty-seven, Julia Altrocchi repeatedly asked her mother why she, Julia, felt so different from other members of the family who were cold, humorless progeny of English forebears. Her mother finally told Julia that she was actually one-quarter Irish. Julia was thrilled and immediately leaped up from her chair and danced an Irish jig! Perhaps this new ethnic revelation sowed the seeds for her later emergence as a humorist.

A second factor in the late onset of her sense of humor was marrying, at the age of twenty-eight in Chicago, Rudolph Altrocchi, Professor of Italian Language and Literature, who was born in Florence, Italy, the son of an American father and a multilingual European mother. He became fluent in English, Italian and French and emigrated to the United States at the age of seventeen, having been registered as an American citizen at birth. With a small inheritance from his father who had suddenly died, he bought a pig farm in Missouri and raised hogs while pondering his future, also learning to speak fluent Pig. He loved pigs, describing them as extremely clever, witty animals. Despite his success at farming for two years, he decided to give it up to continue his education. He became a member of Harvard's Class of 1908 as its only quadri-lingual pig farmer. He loved Harvard and stayed there to take his Ph.D. in Italian in 1914.

Rudolph Altrocchi was a gifted humorist and raconteur. Because of his brilliance in evoking laughter from story-telling, groan-eliciting puns and doggerel poetry, Julia concentrated her talents on serious conversation. She never attempted to be humorous until after Rudolph died in May 1953 at the age of seventy when she was fifty-nine years old. Rudolph had always encouraged her emergence from being a reserved introvert; it was she who chose to be serious.

Once she started making a conscious effort to become funny as a story-teller beginning in 1953, she rapidly burst forth with amazing gusto and success. In a short time she became a very good raconteur, including in the fine art of telling anecdotes on herself, which outstanding wits do so well and where many aspiring humorists often fear to tread.

Co-editor Paul never once heard his mother relate a funny story before 1953 when he was a medical student in Boston. For the next two decades, he can't remember a single occasion when she did *not* make him laugh with her humorous tales. When asked about this change, she always attributed it to the emergence of her "Irish elfish self" and she would immediately start laughing. In the meantime, she read many books on Ireland and traveled there extensively, immensely enjoying the Irish people, their country, their history and their pervading sense of humor.

When the two co-editors decided to work on the Bobolo book, our "authorial research" yielded the following information:

1. Julia never threw away her research notebooks or other research data. There was no inherited material whatsoever about Bobolo Bonomo — no mention of him or the Bobolo book in files, diaries or notebooks.

2. There is no evidence that Bobolo, his family or the Bonomo Country Inn in Alviso, California, ever existed.

3. During the writing of the book, as verified by her older son, John, who lived with Julia from 1952 to 1957 while getting his Ph.D. in Psychology at Berkeley, she never mentioned Bobolo as a real person.

4. Julia arrived in the San Francisco Bay Area in the summer of 1928 when Rudolph became Head of the Department of Italian at the University of California at Berkeley and turned it into the largest and best department in the United States, directing it for nineteen years. In her book, Bobolo dies in May of 1931. In those three years it is extremely unlikely that either she or Rudolph ever encountered Bobolo Bonomo — their social circles and interests were too different. They lived in Berkeley and had no friends or acquaintances in San Jose or Alviso. There is no record that they ever stayed at the Bonomo Country Inn in the hills above San Jose, if it existed.

5. Co-editor Paul lived in the family home from 1931 to 1946 before being sent east to school and never heard mention of "Bobolo," "Bonomo," or any country inn or resort in the southern Bay Area.
6. Julia liked to include explanatory prefaces to elucidate the genesis of her literary works. There was no preface in the Bobolo manuscript.
7. All of Julia Altrocchi's published books were ultra-serious, including: her early poetry; her best work *Snow Covered Wagons,* the tragic story of the Donner Party of 1846–1847, written dramatically in verse; and *Wolves Against the Moon*, a true historical novel of fur-trappers and explorers in the midwest at the time of battles between the French, British and Native Americans during colonial expansion in the 1700's. She wrote several non-fiction books on California, including her history of San Francisco, *The Spectacular San Franciscans,* commissioned by E.P. Dutton, publishers, as part of their series on colorful American cities. She also wrote an epic narrative poem, *Black Boat,* about powerful racial prejudice in the U.S Military in World War II.

In sum, during her seventy-five year writing career beginning at age four, her only humorous literary work is *Bobolo: Man of Mirth.* Our conclusion is that this book derived totally from the imagination of Julia Cooley Altrocchi, driven by her innate Irish humor and joyous approach to living which became so clearly manifest in the last twenty years of her life.

The only alternate motivation we can envision is that after Rudolph's death, she sought a humorous subject to divert herself from the loss of her beloved life-partner. Her marriage of thirty-two years had been extremely successful and happy.

During World War II, Julia decided to improve her already prolific vocabulary by reading the entire *Webster's Dictionary* of more than three thousand pages. To the dinner table five nights a week for more than three years, to expand the brains of her two young sons, she brought interesting examples of unusual words and word origins. The boys found this tradition thought-provoking and memorable but very few such words elicited side-splitting laughter or profound mirth. She was indeed a serious lady until she suddenly burst forth as a humorist at the age of sixty.

Editing the original Bobolo manuscript has been a most pleasant undertaking during the pandemic, punctuated with smiles and laughter at Julia Cooley Altrocchi's creativity and comic bent, an innate talent so long hidden.

Paul Hemenway Altrocchi, MD
Catherine Altrocchi Waidyatilleka, M.Ed.

Honolulu, Hawaii
November 2020

Editors

Dr. Paul Altrocchi is a graduate of Harvard College, Harvard Medical School and Columbia University's New York Neurological Institute. He spent his early career on the full-time faculty of Stanford Medical School, then became Head of Neurology at the Palo Alto Medial Clinic. He completed his career in Oregon. He is a Past President of the American Society of Clinical Neurologists.

A year off from medical school on a Traveling Fellowship in International Health to the South Pacific and Africa provided him with a lifelong hobby, enhanced by a Master's Degree in Public Health from Berkeley and a degree in Tropical Medicine from the University of São Paulo, Brazil. He spent his sabbaticals and many of his vacations working and teaching Neurology in the less developed world.

Since retirement Dr. Altrocchi has lived in Hawaii and has published twenty-four articles and twelve books on the Shakespeare Authorship Question, favoring the authorship of Edward de Vere, 17th Earl of Oxford. Dr. Altrocchi has five daughters and nine grandchildren.

 Catherine Altrocchi Waidyatilleka was raised in Atherton, California. Summer camp introduced her to the charms of new England, where she returned for her university education at Colby College in Waterville, Maine. She majored in English Literature, and was the diver and a sprinter on the swimming team.

During high school and college she spent summers working in Mexico, Honduras, the Caribbean island of Dominica and the South African Kingdom of Lesotho. After two stimulating years teaching English with the Peace Corps in Sri Lanka, where she also became fluent in Sinhala, she spent twelve months earning her Master's Degree in Education at Stanford. She recently earned a second Master's Degree, this time in the new field of Humane Education.

For the past thirty-three years she has taught English and coached diving at 'Iolani School in Honolulu. She lives in the hills of Honolulu with her husband, Nandi. Her two sons graduated from Colorado State University and the University of Richmond.